THE FACELESS ADVERSARY

BOOKS BY THE LOCKRIDGES

—

The Faceless Adversary

BY

FRANCES AND RICHARD
LOCKRIDGE

J. B. LIPPINCOTT COMPANY
Philadelphia   New York

THE FACELESS ADVERSARY

I

John Hayward was thirty-two years and some months old on the early morning of April twenty-fourth. He was five feet eleven inches tall; he weighed a hundred and sixty pounds; he had light brown hair, which was trimmed every two weeks and which he parted on the left side. He was a graduate of Harvard, a lieutenant in the army reserve, unmarried, and assistant to a vice president of the Cotton Exchange National Bank. He had a pleasant face about which there was nothing especially noteworthy.

At twenty minutes of one that Sunday morning John Hayward was, nevertheless, set apart from his fellows—from other well-established (and well set up), youngish executives of promising future and unexceptionable past who lived in Manhattan (and would one day live in one of the better suburbs) and who still, long after graduation, bought suits and shirts at Brooks Brothers. What set John Hayward apart glowed in him. He was happy.

He closed the taxicab door and whistled—not precisely on pitch—a tune from the musical comedy to which he had just taken Barbara. He said good night to the cab driver in a tone so unexpectedly cheerful that the cabbie, by no means a happy man, said, "'Night, Mac," and for a moment looked after him, shaking his head in wonder. Acted, the driver thought, like a man who had maybe just inherited a million dollars.

John Hayward crossed the sidewalk, still whistling softly, and went into the apartment house in which he lived. In the lobby, which was dimly lighted, he ceased to whistle, since one is considerate of sleepers, even if remote. A smile remained on his pleasant face and he thought, of course, of Barbara who, on being asked to marry him, had said she would like to very much. She had said this at a quarter of

7

twelve, sitting beside John on a sofa in the library of her father's house in the East Sixties. John Hayward had not actually been surprised, since he was a man of perception. It was nevertheless astonishing how happy he had suddenly become. He had not known himself to be capable of so much happiness. He had not known he had it in him.

Harry, the night man, sat on a bench by the elevator and said, "Good evening, Mr. Hayward," when John spoke to him. He looked at John Hayward rather intently, but of this John was only vaguely conscious, although he was usually observant. (This had been noted, favorably, at the bank.) At the fifth floor, when Harry opened the door, John said good night and Harry, in a voice which seemed a little louder than was necessary, said, "Good night, Mr. Hayward." John did not notice the loudness of the voice.

John walked down the corridor to his apartment. Again, although without being aware of it, he whistled softly. He put his key in the lock and then, as if they had come out of nowhere, there was a man on either side of him. One of the men was rather short, and noticeably broad of shoulder. The other man was taller. He was thin and his face seemed to droop.

"You're John Hayward?" the shorter man said, in a conversational tone, and entirely without inflection. John, who had been bending a little toward the lock, straightened up. He looked at the shorter man, and then at the other.

"What—" he began.

"Police," the shorter man said. "We'd like a word with you."

A complete blankness invaded John Hayward's mind. He looked at the shorter man again, and then at the other.

"Inside, if you don't mind," the shorter man said. Then he waited. John turned the key in the lock and pushed the door open, and then stood back.

"Go ahead, Mr. Hayward," the shorter man said. "Go ahead in."

John went in, and the two men followed him.

8

"Probably wants to see our shields," the shorter man said, and held a police badge cupped in his hand. "Show him yours, Nate," he said, and the taller man showed him a badge. John looked at the badges, and then again at the men. He shook his head.

"My name's Grady," the shorter man said. "This is Detective Shapiro."

Both of the policemen looked at John Hayward.

"Well," Grady said, "what did you kill her for, Mr. Hayward?"

He did not speak dramatically, or harshly. He spoke merely as if the answer would be one he would find interesting.

The violence of this quietly asked question was like a tearing of the fabric of the mind. Once John Hayward had been standing in a train which slowed for a station and a coupling had broken in the brake hose between two cars of the train, so that at one moment the train was moving and in the same moment was not. John, like others standing in the aisle, had been hurled forward, as if the air had opened in front of him. He had flailed his arms, as others had, clutching for support. It was so now; almost physically so. For an instant he could not see the two men. In that instant the tendons in his hands tightened, as if to grab at some solidity.

And then he saw the men clearly, and knew them to be waiting and John breathed deeply, but without letting that be seen, and said, "I'm afraid I don't know what you're talking about." He said this quite steadily, in a tone no more emphatic than Grady's had been. With that said, he was no longer whirling in unresisting air; with that he was, again, John Hayward, a man well trained to composure, as a banker has need to be. He thought of adding to what he had said, and did not. And now he waited.

"Doesn't know what we're talking about," Detective Grady said to the taller detective. "Just like that, Nate. No idea at all what we're talking about."

They both looked at John Hayward. John made himself say nothing. It was a way one learned. It was a mistake to

9

speak too quickly. It was better not to speak at all. He had said what there was to say and— But then, suddenly, there was a great fear in his mind; a fear which screamed so loudly that he could not hear what Detective Shapiro said in answer, although he could see Shapiro's lips move.

A name screamed in John's mind—*Barbara! Barbara!*

"Thought of something, Mr. Hayward?" Grady said, in the same tone he had used before. "Remembered something?"

He had left her an hour ago—less than an hour ago. She had gone with him to the door of the house. She had kissed him at the door. She had said, "Run along now. But—don't run far." She had held her arms out to him and they had kissed again, not lightly as before. She had held tight to him. She had said, "Don't ever run far," and then, suddenly, pushed him away and looked up at him—

"Who has been killed?" John Hayward said, in an entirely steady voice. "Who are you talking about?"

He knew, from their faces, that they had been waiting for that. He knew that his asking of the question was gratifying to the policemen.

"Who?" he repeated.

Detectives Grady and Shapiro looked at each other. They were evidently satisfied, although Shapiro's face was sad.

"That's a reasonable question, Nate," Detective Grady said. "You can see a man would want—"

"*Tell me!*" John Hayward said. His voice was harsh, strained. "*Who has been killed?*"

"All innocent," Grady said. "Doesn't even know her name. Think he's—" He did not finish. He shook his head. He spoke in a new tone; almost an angry tone. "Nora Evans, Mr. Hayward," he said. "Who'd you think?"

The train started again. The air was palpable again.

"I never heard of Nora Evans," John said.

They looked at him very carefully. They waited, very evidently, for him to go on.

He let them wait.

10

"Looks like he's going to make it hard for everybody," Detective Grady said. "Look that way to you, Nate?"

Detective Shapiro nodded his head, gloomily.

"Nora Evans," Grady said. "Red head. Pretty—up to maybe two-three o'clock. Sure you know her, Mr. Hayward. Well as anybody could."

"No," John said. He kept his voice quite steady. "I didn't know her, officer."

Grady made sounds of tongue and teeth, as at arrant stupidity, or childish stubbornness.

"O.K.," he said. "Any way you want it, Mr. Hayward." He paused. It appeared, quite unconvincingly, that a new method of approach had occurred to him. "Tell you what," he said. "Maybe we can refresh your memory. Think we could do that, Nate?"

"We can try," Detective Shapiro said. "We can always try." But there was no optimism in his voice.

He took a step toward John Hayward. He took hold of John's right arm, pressing the arm hard.

They took him back down the corridor, one walking on either side. They took him down in the elevator, and Harry said, "Jeeze, Mr. Hayward. They—" and was told, abruptly, to hold it. Harry held it, but he shook his head, slowly, from side to side.

Grady sat beside John Hayward in the back seat of a small sedan. It was not far from the apartment house in the Murray Hill district to the city mortuary at Bellevue.

It was warm for April in New York. Even into the New York air some of the freshness of spring had filtered. It was cold in the morgue, and there was a smell of many chemicals mingled. "Evans," Grady said to the uniformed man in the anteroom; who merely nodded, and opened a door, and led them down a corridor—cold, seemingly damp—into a good-sized room. There were several metal tables in the room, and on one there was a body covered by a sheet. The sheet clung a little to the body. Shapiro's hand was heavy, hurrying, on

11

John's arm. It stopped him, with a kind of jerk, by the table. Grady pulled the sheet part way back.

The girl had, as Grady had said, been pretty. She had had red hair—brownish red. The eyes were closed. The face was a little discolored. On the slender throat there were several small wounds, little more than scratches.

"Well?" Grady said. "What d'you say now?"

"No," John said. His voice was steady. "I never saw her before. Is this—" He hesitated. "Was this Nora Evans?"

"That's right," Grady said. "Let's see your hands, Mr. Hayward."

John held his hands out. They were thin, strong hands, long fingered. Grady looked at them.

"About right, I'd say," he said. "Wouldn't you, Nate? Nails about right, too. Marked her up, see, Mr. Hayward? Nails cut into her skin a little. Do that, you know."

"I didn't," John said. "You mean she was strangled?"

Grady sighed, very deeply, lengthily. He shook his head.

"I never saw her before," John said.

"Keep looking," Grady said, and pulled the sheet from the body.

Nora Evans's face had been pretty. Her body was beautiful. It was defenseless under their eyes.

"That ought to help," Grady said.

John looked from the slender, defenseless body. He looked at Grady.

"No," he said. "I never saw her before."

Grady looked at John Hayward across the white body of the murdered girl. He told John to look again, and John looked again. He said, again, "No."

"What's the sense of this?" Grady asked him. "You keep saying the wrong thing. Why don't you just say you didn't kill her?" He looked at Detective Shapiro, beside John. "That's good advice, isn't it, Nate?" Grady said. "Be some sense in that."

Shapiro didn't say anything.

"Well," Grady said, "it's your neck, Mr. Hayward." He

pulled the sheet back over the naked body of the girl named Nora Evans. He said, "All right, let's get going." They went out of the morgue and in the car, across town, to a police station. They took him into a fair-sized room with a wooden table and several wooden chairs, and told him to sit down, and went out and locked the door behind them. There was one window in the room—high up, and barred. After a few minutes Grady came back, carrying a large envelope. "Just put what you've got in your pockets in here," he said, and put the envelope on the table. "We'll keep it for you."

John took things out of his pockets—a billfold with a little over a hundred dollars in it, a key container with five keys, less than a dollar in silver, two subway tokens. He took a fountain pen out of his jacket pocket and a small notebook. He took a folded handkerchief from the breast pocket of his jacket, and a crumpled handkerchief from his right hip pocket. "Never mind," Grady said of the handkerchiefs, and pushed them back. "Might catch cold." John took an almost full package of cigarettes from a pocket, and a Zippo lighter. "You can keep those," Grady told him. "You can keep your watch." He went behind John and ran his hands quickly, not at all roughly, over John's clothing. He was satisfied; he said, "O.K." He said that they'd give him a receipt when they saw what they had, and carried the envelope out of the room, and locked the door after him. John Hayward lighted a cigarette. It tasted of disinfectant.

John looked at his watch. It was still not two o'clock. It had not been an hour since he had put his key in the lock. (It had been only two hours or so since Barbara Phillips had said that she would like very much to marry him. You were whistling a tune and stepped out and—and there was nothing there. And that was senseless.)

It was, of course, a colossal—an indefensible—mistake on the part of some one, or on the part of several. Grady and Shapiro had, he supposed, done only what they had been told to do. The mistake lay elsewhere, lay higher up. Somehow, somewhere, things had got out of order. Since the world

13

was an orderly place, things would, of course, be straightened out. At a few minutes before two o'clock on the morning of Sunday, April twenty-fourth, John Hayward knew that order was persistent in human affairs—he was not convinced of it; he knew it. Mistakes did occur. They were rectified. This one would be. Otherwise, the world became preposterous, and all things in it meaningless, and that, John Hayward knew, was simply not the case.

With a few exceptions so rare as to be unimportant—loose objects falling from tops of buildings was the only example which came at once to mind—the unexpected did not happen to people one knew. (He had not, in fact, known anyone who had been hit by an object falling from the top of a building.) Men and women became ill and died of illness, which was in order, if not in pleasant order. In war—of which John had learned in Korea—men were killed suddenly. But that was part of order, also—hideous, but not unarranged for. In short, the unexpected did not happen.

It had not, at any rate, until that time happened to John and what was happening now, since it was preposterous, would of necessity be brief. What before had happened to John Hayward had been planned, and had occurred according to plan—to his parents' plan first, afterward to his own. He had been sent to Andover; he had gone to Harvard. He had played baseball at Harvard. After graduation, he had spent a summer in Europe with his parents. The following autumn, he had gone to work at the bank. There are few things more orderly than a bank; no place in which mistakes are more painstakingly corrected. In a bank—particularly, of course, in such a bank as the Cotton Exchange—events to come may be anticipated. In a bank, one thing leads, impassively and inevitably, to another, and mistakes of reckoning are made only by depositors.

John was a little surprised, as he waited in the largish room with the barred window for the error which had brought him there to be discovered and corrected, to find the reassuring thoughts as to the orderliness of things invading his mind.

The obvious went without saying. Up to that time it had also gone without thinking.

He heard a sound at the door and sighed slightly in relief. (Until then he had not realized that he was uneasy—annoyed, certainly; in a sense shocked; by a girl's violent death humanly saddened.) The door opened and several men came in. Grady was one of them. A large man with a fat red face, and sharp blue eyes sunk in it, was another. A much younger man with a lean face and a noticeably sharp nose was a third. The lean-faced man wore a sports jacket and a tattersall vest. The fourth man was in uniform.

It wouldn't, John realized at once, take four men to tell him that someone had made a mistake.

The big man with the fat face had an unexpectedly soft voice.

"Now that you've had time to think it over, Mr. Hayward," he said. "Why did you kill the girl?"

"I told Detective Grady—"

The big man shook his head. He said he knew that Mr. Hayward had told Grady.

"What it comes to," he said, "is that you're wasting everybody's time. You're an intelligent man. You ought to see that. Two-timing you, wasn't she?"

"I never saw her in my life," Hayward said. He found that his voice was quite steady, and his mind entirely alert. "Until I saw her body at the morgue," he added.

"No," the big man said. "You shacked up with her. That's the way the army puts it, isn't it? Shacked up with her last —when was it, Tom?"

Tom was Detective Grady. He got a notebook out of his pocket and looked at it, turning several pages before he came to the one he wanted.

"November," he said. "Moved in November fourth. She looked at the apartment—let's see—middle of October. Looked at it a couple of times. Alone the first time. Second time, you were with her, Mr. Hayward. Made a deposit of—" He looked further. "Three hundred thirty. Two months' rent."

John shook his head. "No," he said. "I don't even know what apartment you're talking about. I never saw the girl in my life."

It came back to that. Always, over and over, it came back to that. John's voice grew tired; after a long time he could hardly recognize it as his voice. But his mind held dogged. "I never saw her. You're making some kind of a mistake. You've got me confused with somebody else."

They were patient. They were always patient. There was no limit set to the time they would take. And they were completely confident. That was apparent almost from the beginning. It was apparent in the soft voice of the big man, who was named Miller, who was a detective captain. It was as evident in the light, hard voice of the lean-faced man, who was named Martinelli, and who was from the district attorney's office. The names of the men lodged in John's mind as, during the hours, they spoke to one another—deplored, one to the other, the foolish stubbornness of this man who insisted on denying what was beyond question true.

They explained that. They were very careful to explain that. They told him it was no good to go on denying he had known Nora Evans, that he had rented an apartment for her in, as it turned out—but they did not, explicitly, tell him what they were certain he knew—to be in East Eleventh Street, just beyond Fifth Avenue.

"Say you didn't kill her," Miller said, in his soft voice, leaning toward John. He sat on, bulged over, one of the straight wooden chairs. He leaned forward, his legs spread, a big hand on either big knee. "You got a right to say that. Anybody's got a right to say he didn't kill."

"I didn't know her," John said. "I never saw her alive. How could I have killed her?"

"Maybe you didn't mean to kill her," Miller said, his soft voice gentle, encouraging. "Maybe you were horsing around with her, the way people do sometimes. Maybe you put a

16

hand on her throat to hold her off—something like that. See what I mean? Or maybe she came at you with something—got mad because you were walking out—and all you planned to do was hold her off. Didn't realize how little it takes, sometimes, to kill that way. Sometimes you hit that—what d'they call it, Marty?"

"Carotid sinus," Martinelli said. "Sure, it could have happened that way, Mr. Hayward. Almost amount to an accident if it happened that way."

But it would not amount to that—not to Miller, not to Assistant District Attorney Martinelli. They did not need to tell him that.

"I didn't know her," John said, and they shook their heads at him. They asked him what was the use of saying that.

"Tell you how it could have been," Grady said. "Maybe this was the way it was. Maybe when you went there this afternoon she was already dead. Maybe somebody'd been there earlier—maybe somebody else who figured she was two-timing *him*. See what I mean? Maybe when you found she was dead you got panicky. First idea was to get out of there. Could have been that way."

"Sure," Miller said. "You've got something there, Grady. You—"

"I was never there," John said. "I never saw the apartment. I never saw the girl alive."

They listened. They paid no attention—no real attention. Perhaps he knew about another man? Perhaps Nora Evans had told him about this other man? A man she had known before she met John Hayward? Had parted from? Perhaps a man who had made threats—jealous threats—which she had not taken seriously? Things happened like that. Mr. Hayward must know they happened like that. He would not want to protect this other man—if there was another man.

"She was a pretty girl," Miller said, and his soft voice was sad. "Couldn't have been more than twenty-two, twenty-three. I've got a daughter about that age." He paused. "Makes you think," he added.

17

But John said over what he had said before, and they shook their heads as they had shaken them before. But they did not lose patience. Even Martinelli, of the sharp face, the sharper voice, did not lose patience. They did not threaten—except that the whole mass of their disbelief was in itself a threat. They did not touch him; they did not use harsh lights to torment his eyes. They let him smoke. His mouth grew hot and dry from cigarettes smoked too rapidly, yet he smoked on, hardly realizing what he did. When his lighter failed after an hour or so, Miller provided matches. When, finally, John found his pack empty, and crumpled it and tossed it on the table, Miller took a pack from his pocket and put it within reach.

For more than an hour they told him no more than that the girl was dead, that she had been killed in an apartment in East Eleventh Street, that she had been his girl—finally, that he had killed her. But they would, John began to believe, have been content—for the time content—if he had only admitted that he knew her, that she had been his girl. That he would not admit this, take advantage of one of the alternatives they offered—another man as murderer, murder as an accident—puzzled them. Slowly, he began to realize this. He kept saying the wrong thing. Grady had told him that, across the body of the murdered girl. Miller told him that. Martinelli told him that. It did not, he thought, alter their certainty. It merely puzzled them.

Another man came in after this had gone on for almost two hours. He was named Garfield. He was a lieutenant— "'Lo, lieutenant," Miller said. "Took a while, didn't it?"

Garfield had black hair and black eyes. He was in his middle forties, when he spoke the words came very rapidly, but with sharp precision.

"Says he didn't know her," Miller told Garfield, and Garfield looked at John, with no expression in his eyes. "Says he was never at the apartment."

Garfield took an envelope out of his pocket. He took a piece of paper from the envelope and put it down in front of John.

It was a check. It was drawn on the Riverside National Bank. It was payable to the Applegate-Meyer Realty Corporation. It was for one hundred and sixty-five and no one hundredths dollars. It was signed "John Hayward."

John looked at it, and a kind of numbness invaded his mind. It was, for a moment, as if, between him and reality, there was a pane of glass—a pane of glass invisible, but impenetrable. It was as if his mind pushed at the glass.

They waited.

"It looks like my signature," John Hayward said, in an expressionless voice which was not his own. "I didn't write it. I have no account at that bank." The glass seemed to dissolve. The mistake was there; now they would see the mistake. It might not be until Monday, but then a telephone call would do it. "No," the bank manager would say, "we have no depositor named—"

"For this month's rent," Garfield said. "Reached the office this morning, so they hadn't got around to depositing it." He looked at John, and John shook his head. "Had to get hold of the bookkeeper," Garfield said, and this was an aside to Miller, to Martinelli. "Get him down there."

"Break," Miller said.

"Yes," Garfield said. "A break. Mr. Hayward pays regularly, a few days before the first." He had not looked away from John. "The checks have always cleared, Mr. Hayward," he said. "So you have got an account, evidently. You're a banker. You can see that."

John picked the check up. He held it so the light fell brightly on it. It was a forgery, of course. There would be something— He could not see anything. If he had not known, he would have accepted the signature without question. If he had still worked a teller's window he would have accepted it without question.

"It's a forgery," he said. "Very good. But I didn't write it."

He knew, then. It was not a mistake. It was not anything so disorderly as a mistake. It was a thing prepared; a trap set.

They shook their heads. They seemed to pity him. They

did not even bother to answer him. Garfield picked the check up and put it back in the envelope and put the envelope in his pocket.

"Why did you kill her, Mr. Hayward?" Miller asked, in the same soft voice. "Because she was in the way? Because of Miss Phillips? Because—"

He stopped. John was not listening. It was a trap set by someone. It was a trap set by a murderer—a trap artfully constructed by— His mind whirled. *By whom?* Someone who had reached out at random—put the set trap in a path on which anybody— But it was not that; not as simple as that. By someone who hated him? *Might even kill a girl to spring a trap of hate?* By—

"Listen, Mr. Hayward," Miller said in his soft voice, not even bothering to raise his voice. "Was it because of Barbara Phillips? Because Miss Evans threatened to spill her story if you left her? Spill it to Miss Phillips? And because that would break things up between you and Miss Phillips? Finding out you were keeping this girl while you were—"

"No," John said. "I wasn't keeping Miss Evans. I never—"

"The wrong thing," Miller said. "You keep on saying the wrong thing." But, still, there was only patience in his voice. "You've been seeing a lot of Miss Phillips. From what we hear. Say you two make a very—"

For the first time, John interrupted.

"You've been to her?" he said. "Been badgering her? Her father?"

Miller looked at Lieutenant Garfield.

"Not yet," Garfield said. "You wouldn't like that, would you, Mr. Hayward? With Mr. Phillips so high up at the bank. In a position to push you along? Or the other way around." He paused. "Would have been," he added.

"And," Miller said, "with the Phillipses having all that money."

John merely shook his head. It was true enough. Martin Phillips was a senior vice president at the bank. Martin Phillips had a lot of money. Those things had nothing to do with him and Barbara. But it would have been impossible for John to have said this to Miller and Garfield; said it to be noted down by the man in uniform, the police stenographer.

"You were going to marry Miss Phillips?" Miller said.

John answered steadily.

"Yes," he said, "I am going to marry Miss Phillips."

They were puzzled again, he thought, and this time by the change of tense. Because they were quite certain he had killed a girl, and so was not going to marry anyone. There was more to the trap into which he had walked, whistling— not quite on pitch—a tune from a show to which he had taken his girl. There had to be.

II

THERE WAS MORE. There was the matter of two white shirts.

They were quite ordinary shirts. They were made of a good quality of broadcloth; they had collar points of moderate length. They came from Brooks Brothers. He was shown the shirts about an hour after he had been shown the check on the Riverside National Bank, Murray Hill Branch.

It had grown hot in the room, and the room was filled with smoke. John began to cough, from the smoke in the room and from the hot smoke he drew into his throat and lungs. They waited while he coughed. At a nod from Miller, the uniformed man went out of the room and came back with a pitcher of water and several glasses. The water was warmish from the tap, but John drank thirstily.

"Maybe," Miller said, "you'd like a cup of coffee? A hamburger, maybe?" He paused, briefly. "We don't want you to say we tried to wear you down," he added. "We're not trying to do that."

"Not that way," John said. "No, I don't want anything to eat."

"However you want it," Miller said. "Grady, want to get those things?"

Grady got up and went out. He came back with something around which brown paper was folded. He took the paper off and handed two shirts to Miller. Miller put them on the table in front of John Hayward. John looked at them without touching them. They were stretched over laundry cardboard.

"Yours, aren't they?" Miller said, in his soft, patient voice.

"I don't know," John said. "I wear shirts like these."

"Yes," Miller said. "You're wearing one now, Mr. Hayward. They're your shirts." John looked at him. "Laundry marks," Miller said. He pointed to the mark on the inside of the collar. The mark was "HH201." "Your mark," Miller told him.

23

It was vaguely familiar to John. He could not, without prompting, have said how the laundry marked his shirts, but "HH201" was probably the way. Anyway, they would have checked on that.

"All right," John said. "Probably they're mine."

"Sure," Miller said. "Two or three pairs of shorts, too. In Miss Evans's apartment. What did you want to kill the girl for, Mr. Hayward?"

"No," John said. "It's the way I said. I never knew the girl. I was never in the apartment. You see what it is?"

Miller shook his big head, sadly.

"It's no good," he said. "No good saying we're framing you. What would we want to frame you for? What would we have against you?" He shook his head again, slowly—very slowly. "We just work here," he said. "That's all there is to it, Mr. Hayward."

"Not you," John said. "I don't say that."

"Not anybody," Miller said. "You kept the girl. You killed the girl. Simple as that. Probably because she was going to spill things to Miss Phillips."

"I'd be a louse," John said. "Do I look like a louse?"

"No," Miller said. "You look pretty much like anybody. But—sure you're a louse. Not that I give a damn, or Marty here. Or anybody. How you explain about the shirts?"

"Whoever killed the girl," John said, "rented the apartment for her. Is doing all this—did do all this—to put it on to me."

"Oh," Martinelli said. "For the love of God, Mr. Hayward!"

"He's got a right," Miller said. "He's got a right to say anything. Why would anybody do that, Mr. Hayward? Because you know where the body's buried? Because you've been stealing somebody's toys? You tell us, Mr. Hayward."

"I don't know why," John said. "Somebody did. I never knew the girl."

They all listened. They shook their heads. Miller looked at his watch, and then John looked at his. It was ten minutes of five.

24

"No," Miller said. "We'll go on for a while. Unless you've decided—"

John shook his head. He lighted another cigarette from Miller's pack, using Miller's matches.

"So we don't make any mistake," Garfield said, "because we don't want to make a mistake, what were you doing yesterday afternoon?"

He said this rapidly—very distinctly, but very rapidly. Adjusted to the slow, soft speech of Miller, almost intolerably weary, John's mind lagged for an instant. He hesitated. And he could see in their faces, reaction to his hesitancy. In spite of himself, there was a kind of quiver in his brain. But then it was gone.

"I asked—" Garfield began, and John spoke quickly, and steadily. "What I was doing yesterday afternoon," he said. "I heard you."

They waited. John did not hurry, but he did not, in the sense they wanted, hesitate. He spoke as one thinking, remembering, seeking exactitude. He had had lunch at the Harvard Club. Was that where they wanted him to begin?

"Go ahead," Garfield said. "You had lunch."

He had gone to the club alone, with no plans before evening. He said merely that he had gone alone. He had stopped at the bar, and he had met an acquaintance at the bar. A man named Curtis—Alfred Curtis. After a drink—

"Two drinks," Garfield said. "That's right, isn't it?"

"If you know all this—" John began, and checked himself. "Two drinks," he said. "It was Saturday."

"Sure," Miller said. "Since it was Saturday."

But somehow, obscurely, the correction put him in the wrong. It was unfair that it should. John felt resentment beginning in his mind. He forced his mind to coolness.

He and Alfred Curtis, after two drinks each, had had lunch. They wouldn't care what they'd eaten—

"All the same," Garfield said. "Just to keep things straight."

John had had consommé. A minute steak. Au gratin potatoes. Coffee.

"And a salad," Garfield said. "Not that it makes any difference."

Curtis had had—

"All right," Garfield said. "When was this? When you ate?"

It had probably been one-thirty, or a quarter of two, when they had begun to eat. It was probably around two-thirty, or a few minutes later, when they finished coffee and cigarettes. Curtis had told him about a place in the West Indies where Curtis had spent several weeks during the winter. John had expressed envy. The bank was conservative. Holidays were for summertime, for those under the rank of vice president.

"Then?"

Then they had walked through the club, and out of it into Forty-fourth Street. John had left Curtis waiting for a cab. John had gone home and spent the rest of the afternoon at his apartment.

He stopped, because Garfield was shaking his head.

"Sure," John said, "that's—"

"Man named Woodson," Garfield said. " 'Pit' Woodson, they call him. You've left him out. Why'd you leave him out, Mr. Hayward?"

John had forgotten Pit Woodson—P. I. T. Woodson. He started to say that that was very easy; that, to most people it was even very desirable. He did not say either thing.

"I'd forgotten that," John said. "We did run into Woodson going out. He wanted us to stay around and make up a table of bridge."

"Yes," Garfield said. "So he told us. And—you told him you couldn't. *Because you had a date.* Remember that, Mr. Hayward?"

"I don't—" John began, and stopped because probably he had. It was the sort of thing you told Pit Woodson; it was the sort of thing that a great many men told Pit Woodson, often even before he had had time to ask them to help make up a table of bridge. Men said, with the utmost cordiality, "Hi, Pit," and sometimes even, when their consciences were tender, "Hi, Pit old man." And then, as Pit Woodson started to open his mouth, they said, "Got to be running along. Late already." And ran.

"Very likely I did," John said.

"But you didn't have a date, you say? Not with the Evans girl?"

"Not with anybody," John said. "If I told him that—" He paused. "Well," he said, "poor old Pit is a God-awful bore."

He had phrased it badly. He had spoken too intimately; it was as if he had sought to bring Miller and Garfield, Martinelli and Grady, into a companionship of understanding. And Pit was, after all, a member of the club.

But they merely looked at him, their faces neither accepting nor rejecting. The police stenographer made a note in the book in front of him, and then waited, his pencil point touching the paper. He did not look at John at all.

"About a quarter of three, say, you left the club," Garfield said, after the pause had lengthened. "Took a cab to your apartment? Got there in—what? Five minutes? Ten? About three o'clock, say?"

"No," John said. "It was later than that. Three-thirty. Probably a quarter of four. You see—I didn't take a cab. Walked."

They looked at him. Miller shook his head.

"You could walk it in fifteen minutes," he said. "It would be easy to walk it in fifteen minutes."

"I didn't go straight to the apartment," John said. "I walked a way up the avenue—and over and down Madison. I didn't hurry."

They waited briefly. Then Miller said, "Why did you do that, Mr. Hayward?"

"I felt like walking," John said.

But that had not really been all of it. He had walked slowly, in the spring air. He had felt like walking. He had felt fine. He had stopped to look in the windows of Black Starr & Gorham and had crossed the avenue to look in a window at Cartier's. He had walked as far uptown as Fifty-seventh Street and at the corner had looked in Tiffany's win-

27

dows. He had almost gone into Tiffany's, but in the end had not.

He had been thinking about a ring, and had decided against buying a ring. In the end he wondered how he had ever thought of buying a ring that afternoon, and having it in a pocket to pull out proudly if he was given cause for pride. When he pictured the scene, he realized how entirely presumptuous he had thought of allowing himself to be. (Like a salesman, with an order book; with an injunction to sign here.) It would be the crassest possible way of taking Barbara for granted—of revealing that he took her for granted.

So in the end he had walked through Fifty-seventh and then down Madison, and he had not looked in any more jeweler's windows. But he had taken his time—walked bareheaded in the soft sunshine and thought of the future, which had looked then very good indeed. He had made plans, as one should who contemplates marriage; and that even when the world seems rickety. (But it was only in the largest sense, almost in an academic sense, that the world did seem rickety. It would somehow be shored up; order would, in some fashion, finally assert itself.)

They did not say anything.

"That's all," John Hayward said. "It was a pleasant afternoon. I felt like walking."

"Evidently," Garfield said. "You got in about ten of four."

"I suppose, then," John said, and his voice rasped, but was entirely steady, "that it was some time about then the girl was killed? During that hour?" He pinned it down. "Between a little before three and sometime around four?"

Miller and Garfield looked at each other. They looked at Martinelli, from the district attorney's office.

"About then," Martinelli said. "May as well tell him, lieutenant. He doesn't seem to get the idea, somehow."

At a quarter of three, or thereabouts, Nora Evans had been alive. She had been alive, and carrying yellow daffodils wrapped in a cone of paper, and had been waiting in the

28

lobby of the apartment house in East Eleventh Street for the automatic elevator to come down. The elevator had come down carrying another tenant, who knew Miss Evans by sight —and just to speak to—and had said, "Good afternoon. Such a pretty afternoon," and then, as an afterthought, "Such pretty flowers." Nora Evans had smiled. ("Such a sweet girl, I'd always thought," Mrs. Maude Apfel, who was the outbound tenant, said. "Of course, I hadn't had any idea she was—*that* kind.") Miss Evans had said, "Yes, aren't they?" and got into the elevator. So she was alive then.

She was dead, on the floor of her living room, at about four-ten. She had been wearing only a thin robe, and as she fell ("or in the struggle. Was that it, Mr. Hayward?") the robe had fallen open, so that she lay naked on the floor, except for her sleeve-covered arms. She had been found so by a part-time maid, colored, named Bertha Johnson. Bertha Johnson had notified the police.

"Part-time cleaning woman," Garfield said. "Worked for several people in the neighborhood. Four to six for Miss Evans, Tuesday, Thursday and Saturday. But you knew about that, Mr. Hayward."

"No," John said. "I don't know about that."

He was told, but without conviction, to have it his own way.

Nora Evans had been strangled. The pressure needed in manual strangulation varies greatly. Some die very quickly, when hands are on their throats. Nora Evans had.

But there had been marks. Nails had dug into soft skin. From measurements, the murderer had been a man. He had had long-fingered, strong hands.

Garfield looked at John's hands, and Miller looked at them. John kept his long-fingered hands quite steady.

The murderer's nails had been of medium length, probably extending just beyond the flesh of the finger tips. John held his own hands out, then, still keeping them steady. The nails were cut shorter than that.

"Sure," Garfield said. "We see them, Mr. Hayward. Gave

29

yourself a manicure when you got home, didn't you? Before you went on this other date?"

John merely shook his head.

"She'd been taking a bath," Garfield said. "The Evans girl had. Bathroom was still steamy when the cleaning woman got there. Bath towel wet. Looks like she hadn't expected you right then, Mr. Hayward. Maybe didn't expect you at all. Was that it?"

John said nothing.

"If that's the way he wants it, he's got a right," Miller said.

The assistant medical examiner had not reached the apartment until a little after five. By that time, it could be determined only that the girl had been dead between an hour and two hours, probably nearer two hours.

"You see how it is," Garfield said. "You got a cab—"

"No," John said.

"He's got a right," Miller said.

"O.K.," Garfield said. "You could have got a cab. You like it better that way? You could have got a cab at the Harvard Club say about—oh, make it three o'clock. You could have got down to Eleventh Street in maybe ten minutes. Saturday afternoon. Not as much traffic as usual. Kill the girl in ten minutes—make it fifteen. Get a cab to your place. Get there about a quarter of four. Like you say. Like the elevator man says."

John shook his head.

"You mean there's something wrong with it?" Miller said. "Mean the lieutenant here's got the times wrong?"

"I mean I did what I said. Walked a while."

"But the times are all right? You admit that, don't you?"

"It could have been done that way," John said. His voice, to his own ears, sounded strangely without life. "Maybe it was. Not by me."

Miller sighed. He looked at Garfield, at Martinelli. Martinelli shrugged; Garfield shook his head.

"The way you say it," Miller said. "You were framed. That's the line you're taking." John did not answer. "All right," Mil-

30

ler said. "This man who framed you. How'd he know you wouldn't be some place with a lot of people? Have an alibi we couldn't break down?"

"I don't know," John said. "He must have known."

They kept for a long time to that point. Over and over they asked him, always patiently, always skeptically, what amounted to the same question. He said he had been conspired against—been "framed." Then whoever had framed him must have known that, for the period during which the girl was killed, he had no proof that he could not have been the killer. Then, how did this man who was framing him know that?

They varied the form of the question. They offered him suggestions. Had he told anyone at the club that he was going to walk to his apartment, and not walk there directly? Had someone followed him for a time, until the aimlessness of his direction became evident? John did not know. He said he did not know. He could not remember he had told anyone of his plans. It had not really been a plan. It had been—

Miller asked the questions. Then Martinelli asked them. Then Garfield asked them. Once or twice, but only once or twice, Grady asked a question. They did not hurry him. There were pauses between the questions, apparently to give him time to think of answers—to change answers. But, as time went on, the questions seemed to pulsate in his mind, as blood pulsates through an artery. Was it this way? Was it *this* way? How did this man know? Did you tell someone? And always, there was disbelief in the questions, and in the voices. Utter disbelief—and utter patience.

Weariness dragged at John's mind. He could not keep his mind alert. There was a dullness in his thoughts which was almost a physical pressure—on his eyes, on the cords of his neck. He began to find it hard to remember which of the men was which; it began to seem that the questions came all from one man with different voices, and a man he could no longer clearly see—a man who wavered dimly in a smoky turbulence of air.

But still, as if from a great distance, he answered the questions—answered them dully, but stubbornly. When the men (who were one man) went to other things, he answered doggedly. How did he explain the shirts? How did he explain the check? How did he explain— Again, the questions were over and over repeated. "I don't know. I can't explain. Somebody has made these things look the way they do. I never saw the girl before. I never—"

Then there was what seemed a long time without questions. The men still were there. They still looked at him and he still, through strained, aching eyes, looked back at them. He watched their mouths, to see if their lips moved, if they spoke and he could not hear.

"All right," he heard Miller say, in his soft voice, from far off. "All right. We're getting nowhere now. Give him a place to sleep, Grady. You want to sleep a while, Mr. Hayward?"

John went with Grady, to a place to sleep. It was only when they wakened him, after what seemed a few minutes and was actually about three hours, that he fully realized he had slept in a cell, with a heavy door locked on him. It was the detective named Shapiro who wakened him and told him he could send out for breakfast, if he wanted breakfast. John sent out for breakfast and cigarettes and when food came— apparently from a near-by lunchroom, coffee in a cardboard container, egg sandwich on a cardboard plate—he drank coffee and ate the sandwich. He lighted a cigarette.

His mind was clear again. A certain resilience had come back to it. Toward the end of the questioning, he thought, I must have been in what they call shock. Briefly, but with a sudden coldness of the mind, he wondered whether, in that long period when consciousness wavered, he had said any of the condemning things they had been trying to get him to say. But then, as suddenly, he was certain he had not. He smoked and waited for them to come back, and was wary and alert as a cat is when dogs circle it.

It was Shapiro who came back, and opened the cell door and did not close it. Shapiro looked at him sadly.

He said, "Feeling better, now?" and when John nodded, Shapiro said there was nothing like a cup of coffee.

"Not like this one," John said, tasting the flavor of soaked cardboard still in his mouth, meeting Shapiro halfway. Shapiro smiled dimly and said Mr. Hayward had something there. Then he said they wanted Mr. Hayward should go on a little ride with them, and that maybe he'd want to clean up first. He waited until John came out of the cell and then, walking beside him, but a step behind, not touching him but evidently ready to touch him, directed John to a small washroom off a room which held several desks, with men at two of the desks. John had never seen them before. They looked at him, as he went through the room. They looked at him as if they planned to remember his face.

Shapiro brought John an electric razor and, when John said he had never used one, Shapiro said, without emphasis, that that was funny, but did not say why it was funny. He showed John how to use the razor, and John did, finding the process awkward but more effective than he had supposed it would be. He washed and put back on the shirt he had worn the night before. It did not feel clean. There was nothing to do about his suit, in which he had slept. (I never slept in my clothes before, John thought.) He felt, momentarily, at a disadvantage and then that, under the circumstances, there could be no disadvantage more trivial.

With Shapiro still beside him, and a step—or half a step—behind, he went back through the room with the desks. Grady was at one of them, now, and stood up, and walked on the other side of John. They went out of the station house into the sun. It was another pleasant, early spring day. They got into a car, Shapiro behind the wheel and John and Grady in the back seat. They did not drive far. They stopped midway of a block in East Eleventh Street, in front of an apartment house which was neither very new nor very old.

"Look familiar, Mr. Hayward?" Grady asked, as they got out.

33

"The answer's the same," John said. "I never saw it before. I suppose this is where the girl lived?"

Neither of them answered, except that Shapiro nodded. They went across the sidewalk and into the lobby of the building. It was carpeted, not large. Toward the rear a big man—a softly fat man in a blue shirt open at the throat and khaki trousers—was running a vacuum cleaner over the carpet. He stopped the cleaner when they went in. It was dim in the lobby, but enough daylight came through the door behind, and fell on the man's face, for John to see that he had never seen the man before—and that the man needed a shave.

The man looked at the two detectives. Then he looked at John Hayward.

"That's him," the man said. "About the time I said. A little while after three."

"You're sure, Pedersen?" Grady said. "You wouldn't want to make a mistake."

"That's him," the fat man said. "Saw him just as plain as I'm seeing him now. I was standing right about here." He moved a step forward and continued to look at John. "Think I don't know what I saw?" he asked. His voice was querulous. It was, John thought, the voice of a man who felt himself too often unfairly doubted.

"If you say you saw me—" John said, and Grady interrupted him.

"All right," Grady said. "We know what you're going to say. We'll go up, now."

They waited for John to move. He looked around the lobby and saw the door of an elevator. But Grady had already moved toward it. He pressed a button and the door opened and he went into the elevator. John followed him, and then Shapiro. Again the two men waited, and then John realized that he was closest to the row of buttons which controlled the automatic elevator.

"All right," Grady said, "let's get going."

They waited again. John knew what they waited for.

"Which floor is it?" he asked.

34

"Smart cooky," Grady said, and reached around him and pressed the button numbered "5."

"I suppose," John said, "the man downstairs—the janitor or whatever he is—says he saw me come in yesterday afternoon?"

"That's right," Grady said. "About three-fifteen. Thereabouts."

"He's lying," John said.

"Oh," Grady said, "for God's sake, Mr. Hayward. Why?"

The elevator stopped. The door opened. John stepped out first and waited, just beyond the door.

"All right," Grady said. "You made your point. You don't know what floor. You don't know it's apartment 5-B. This way, Mr. Hayward."

There was a uniformed patrolman outside the door of apartment 5-B. He opened the door for them. He had, John thought, been waiting for them.

There was a small, railed foyer just inside the door. From it, they went down two steps into the living room. The arrangement was familiar. Some years before, John remembered, the "sunken" living rooms had been popular, at least among people who build apartment houses. John had been in a good many apartments almost identical with this. (You could "dine" on the foyer platform. Apartments like this had a name. He could not remember the name.)

"Familiar?" Grady said.

"I've never been here before," John said.

Near the center of the living room there was, in chalk, the rough outline of a human body. The arms of the body had been, apparently, flung out.

"Yes," Grady said, "that's where she was lying. Her hair was a little damp around the edges. Hadn't got it all in the shower cap. Remember that, Mr. Hayward? Hair was a little darker where it was wet. She say anything when she saw you were going to kill her, Mr. Hayward? Try to scream, maybe?"

John looked at the chalked outline. He remembered the slender white body on the table in the morgue.

"Or didn't she know soon enough?" Grady said. "Maybe she thought you were going to make love to her. Was that the way it was?"

It might have been that way, John thought. A girl hurrying toward her lover. Not caring if, as she hurried, the light robe opened from her body. And thinking the strong hands held out toward her were still a lover's hands.

"It's no good, Grady," John said. "I wasn't the one who killed her."

"Rented the apartment," Grady said. "Came here yesterday afternoon about the time she was killed. Couldn't let her mess up your marrying the boss's daughter."

"No," John said, steadily.

"Come here, Mr. Hayward," Grady said. He walked across the room, across the chalked outline. John walked around the place where the girl had died. Grady stood by a table. There were daffodils on it in a vase. There was a framed photograph.

Grady pointed at the photograph—an enlarged snapshot—a snapshot of John Hayward, dressed (apparently) for tennis; a snapshot of John smiling, his eyes crinkled a little, with just a suggestion that the sun was on them. The background was hazy, out of focus.

They did not hurry him. They merely watched him, and, knowing himself watched, he tried to keep from showing in his face the swirling confusion in his mind. But he could feel that there was a fixity in the expression of his eyes; he could feel the muscles around his eyes tightening, setting in tightness.

"Well," Grady said finally, "a picture of you, isn't it? You don't say it isn't a picture of you?"

John was not certain of his voice; he was not certain of anything. Questions pounded in his mind. He shook his head. He couldn't say it wasn't a picture of John Hayward. (A picture taken—*where? when? And—who had taken it?*)

"You got an explanation?" Grady said. "You never saw this

girl. You were never in the apartment. And she had your picture. Stood it up here on the table so she could—"

He stopped. John was still shaking his head. He hardly heard Grady over the pounding of the questions in his mind —the roaring of doubt in his mind. *Are you sure?* something demanded in his mind, shouted in his mind. *Were you never here before?* When you stood on the platform of the foyer you felt the place familiar. Because it was like other apartments of a common kind? Or—*because you have been here before? Have forgotten you were here before?*

Fantasy of doubt swirled in his mind. Surely it was fantasy. It was not—it was mad to think it might be—that he had lived this other life and, somehow, because of some slippage of the mind, forgotten he had lived it. Had known the girl. Had—*killed the girl.* And that his mind, recoiling from the decision it had made, from the act itself, had blotted out, in a frantic effort to hide, all the part of his life which had led up to this unbearable horror.

The mind is strange, John thought. Already, in these hours, I have discovered the strangeness of the mind—have learned that order is not certain; that logic is a façade only. Because all the logic points—

It was as if the swirling fear, the nightmare in his mind, had been a bubble, and suddenly the bubble broke. His mind moved slowly, heavily, back to what was real. (Only a flicker remained; only the echo of a question. Are you certain? Are you certain beyond all doubt?)

"The murderer must have put it there," John said, his voice low, each word spoken carefully.

Grady laughed.

III

THEY TOOK HIM from the living room into a bedroom with twin beds. They asked him whether the room did not refresh his memory. They took him into the bathroom, and pointed to a big bath towel which lay huddled on the floor. Nora Evans had dried herself on the towel, stepping hurriedly from the bath. She had dropped the towel on the floor, in her haste. Grady bent and touched it with the tips of his fingers. "Still a little damp," he said. John said nothing.

Grady opened a medicine cabinet. He pointed to an electric razor on one of the shelves. "Yours, isn't it?" he said, and then John said, "No," and, to Shapiro, "I told you I'd never used one."

"That's right," Shapiro said. "That's what you told me."

"You could see I wasn't familiar with it," John said.

"That's right," Shapiro said. "That's the way it looked."

They took him into a small kitchen off the living room. There was a breakfast table there. "Used to stay to breakfast, probably," Grady said. John shook his head.

They took him back into the bedroom and opened a large closet, with a girl's clothes hanging in it. "Things you bought her, aren't they?" Grady said, and John did not answer.

Grady pointed to a bathrobe, hanging on a hook in the back wall of the closet. "Yours, isn't it?" he said. This time, John said, "No," and Grady merely shrugged. There probably wasn't, John thought, anything to connect him with the bathrobe. That was why they had left it there; why Grady did no more than shrug. That was something. Obviously, it wasn't much.

They took him out of the apartment, and down in the elevator. The fat man and his vacuum cleaner were gone from the small lobby. Presumably, John thought, the fat man had been told to be there at a certain time, had left afterward to go about whatever affairs he had to go about.

They went back to the station house and John Hayward, white, age thirty-two years, was booked on suspicion of homicide. He was fingerprinted. He was told that, now, he could make a telephone call, and a booth was pointed out to him. He reached into empty pockets, and Shapiro gave him a dime. He went into the booth and put the dime in the slot and started to dial the number of the one person he wanted to talk to. But he dialed only the exchange letters and numeral, and then hung the receiver up. The dime rattled into the metal pocket at the bottom of the instrument and John took it out and gave it back to Shapiro.

"Don't answer," John said. "I'll try again later."

They took him back to the cell, then, and locked him into it. He sat on the cot for a time, shielding his eyes with his hands, trying to make his mind work. Then he lay back on the cot and went to sleep, and, though he slept in a turmoil of dreams, he could not, when he wakened, remember more of them than a montage of faces. He could not remember the faces.

Some sound awakened him. He looked at his watch, and found it was after five o'clock. They had left him alone for hours—for almost seven hours. For a moment, between sleep and wakefulness, he had a fear—which he knew to be irrational even while it flared in his mind—that they had forgotten him—locked him up and forgotten him. In that instant, he had a great impulse to stand at the locked door and beat on it. But that passed as quickly as it had come. He sat on the cot, and lighted a cigarette, and his mind was much clearer than it had been. His belief in logic, in essential order, crept back.

It was not a mistake. That was evident, now. This was something which had, deliberately, been done to him—something which had been thought out, carefully, step by step, from first conception to the final crushing force of hands on a girl's throat. Something which had been done to him, and to a slender, pretty girl, who might have thought, in the instant before she knew, that the hands were lover's hands. (It was planned. Remember that. *Hold to that.*)

For, if a thing is planned, thought out, the plan can be discerned. The course of the thought can be retraced. That was what he had to do. Because—and this, now, was entirely clear —they had enough, had been given enough. They had the proof, made up of little things, and big things. It was proof of a lie, but it could be proof enough. Against it, he had only the nakedness of denial. He must have more.

Shapiro opened the door. He asked John if he was getting hungry, and John found he was. Once more he "sent out"— actually, Shapiro made a telephone call for him—to the lunchroom and got back more cigarettes, and tasteless food which he ate hungrily. When he had finished, Shapiro came back and said the captain wanted to see him.

The captain was Miller. He was alone at a desk in a small office. Miller was very broad behind the desk. He was looking at papers, and then putting them in baskets.

He continued to do this for several minutes after John had come into the office, and Shapiro had closed the door, leaving him alone with Miller. Then Miller looked up and said, "Sit down, Mr. Hayward," and looked at several more papers. He wore glasses while he looked at the papers. Then he took the glasses off and looked at John.

"Well," he said, "you've had time to think things over. To see where you stand."

"You've all made it clear where I stand," John said.

To that, Miller said, "Good." Then he said, "The boys have treated you all right? Haven't pushed you around?"

John said the boys had been all right.

"Just doing what we're hired to do," Miller said. "You're a reasonable man. You see that."

"All right," John said.

"Then why the hell," Miller said, "supposing you're a reasonable man, do you stick to this god-damn' crummy story?"

41

He said this without raising, without in any way changing, his soft voice.

"Because there isn't any other story," John said.

Miller tilted back in his chair. He looked at John for what seemed a long time. Then he told John he didn't get it.

"We give you outs," he said. "We give you a line. We don't promise anything, but we give you a line. You're scuffling with the girl, the way people do sometimes, and you choke her, but don't mean to. Then you get panicky. What's the matter with that?"

"Nothing," John said. "Only, it didn't happen. I never saw the girl alive."

"Or," Miller said, "maybe the girl came at you with something. When she found out you were going to ditch her. A knife, maybe. Hell, I don't know. All you meant to do was hold her off. What's the matter with that?"

John merely shook his head.

"I don't say I'd believe it," Miller said. "But somebody might. Nobody was there but you two. How'd anybody know what happened? I've seen juries swallow more than that."

"No," John said.

"You think maybe I'm trying to trap you," Miller said. "You've heard that people in a jam like yours ought to just clam up." He paused. John said nothing. "All right," Miller said, "say I am trying to trap you. I don't say I'm not. All the same, I'm giving you an out. Showing you where there *is* an out. This other way—what chance have you got? You ought to see that. Look, we know you were keeping the Evans girl. We know you want to marry this other girl. We know you went to the apartment yesterday afternoon. Look—that much we *know*." For the first time there was emphasis in the soft voice. "Why don't you give yourself a break?"

He had leaned forward with his hands on the desk top. Now he tilted back again in his chair. The chair creaked.

"I never—" John began, and stopped. "There's not much use in saying it again, is there?"

"No," Miller said.

42

"If you're as sure as you say," John said, "why don't you just let it ride?"

For some seconds, Miller merely looked at him. "I'm damned if I know," Miller said then, and the chair squeaked down. Miller pressed a button on his desk, and almost at once Shapiro opened the door. "Put him back," Miller said.

John stood up. "I've got a telephone call coming," he said.

"Let him make his call," Miller said to Shapiro, not looking at John.

* * *

John Hayward (age thirty-two, banker by profession, resident of East Thirty-sixth Street, City of New York) was arraigned in Felony Court on Monday, April 25, as a material witness to the murder of Nora Evans (age early twenties, resident of East Eleventh Street.) He was ordered held in $20,000 bail. The proceedings were brief, perfunctory—and to John Hayward, entirely puzzling.

"Why?" he asked his attorney. His attorney, reached by telephone the evening before just as he was about to leave for a cocktail party, said he was damned if he knew. He said, "I told you, Johnny, this isn't my line of country." Richard Still, associate of the firm of Laughton, Murphy and Wahlstein, added that he had never been in a magistrate's court before in his life and repeated that he had told John that. He added that he didn't think anybody connected with Laughton, Murphy and Wahlstein had been in a magistrate's court in his—or her, as the case might be—life.

"All the same," John said, "you are a lawyer. Why material witness? They booked me for murder."

"Suspicion of homicide," Still said. "Comes to the same thing, or near enough. I suppose the D. A. changed his mind —or the cops got him to change his mind."

"Why?"

"I don't know," Still said again. "And, if I were you, I

43

wouldn't insist on finding out. A material witness can get bailed out. Homicide, you stay in."

Richard Still was Harvard. He was thirty-three years old. He was close to six feet tall and he weighed in the neighborhood of a hundred and sixty pounds. He had light brown hair, which was cut short, and not parted. He had a pleasant face and a pleasant manner and he got his clothes at Brooks Brothers. Nobody he knew had ever, before, been accused of murder. What it came to—you didn't know people who got accused of murder. Or were suspected of homicide.

His voice had betrayed this on the telephone; his manner betrayed it now. And John Hayward, to his own surprise—and even slightly to his own bewilderment—was faintly amused.

"I know it's off your beat, Dick," he said. "You were the only lawyer I could think of offhand."

"Sure," Still said. "Sure, Johnny."

"You can arrange about the bail?"

"Sure," Richard Still said. "That I can do. Take an hour or so. Then—" He paused. "Look, Johnny," he said, "you need somebody in the criminal end. You realize that? It's not that I—"

"You're not on the hook, Dick," John Hayward said, and there was still a faint flicker of amusement in his mind. (And it was a hell of a time to be amused.) "You fix it about bail."

It was almost noon, then. In Shapiro's custody, John went back to the station house to wait. (As they walked from the court into the sun, flashlight bulbs spurted all around.) At the station house he was not this time put in a cell. He waited in the room where, the night before, he had endlessly answered the same question. He assumed that the door was locked, but he did not try it to find out. Again food was brought from the lunchroom, and more cigarettes.

It was two o'clock when Shapiro, and this time Grady was with him, opened the door. Grady carried a brown envelope, and spilled from it to the table John's keys and wallet, his notebook and fountain pen. "You owe us for the food," Grady

44

said. "Breakfast yesterday, dinner last night, breakfast this morning. Three packages of cigarettes. Three seventy-five." He looked at a slip of paper in his hand. "That's right," he said. "They charge for room service."

John took four dollar-bills from his billfold. Grady gave him back a quarter. John started to put the billfold in his pocket.

"Count it," Grady said. "See it's all there."

John counted it. Since he had not known within ten dollars or so what he had had, the careful counting was pointless. He did not say so. He said it was all right.

"Then sign this," Grady said, and John signed a receipt.

"And away you go," Shapiro said.

"Oh," Grady said, "we'll be seeing him, Nate. We'll be seeing Mr. Hayward."

Detective Nathan Shapiro said sadly, that he shouldn't wonder.

The April day was still bright, still warm. John blinked for a moment in the light. He got a cab and went to his apartment house, and up in the elevator. (The day operator said, "Afternoon, Mr. Hayward," in a voice without any expression whatever—and looked at him with widened, unbelieving eyes.) John put the key in the lock, and nobody stopped him, and went into his small apartment and locked the door after him. Mail had been stuck under the door, and John picked it up carefully and put it on a table without looking at it. Methodically, in the bedroom, he took things out of the pockets of the suit he had been wearing and put them, in orderly fashion, on the chest of drawers. In a jacket pocket, there were the stubs of two theater tickets. He tore those into small pieces and put the pieces in the wastebasket.

He went into the bathroom and showered, and after that he shaved, feeling the smooth certainty of the sharp blade on his face. After he had finished shaving, had dressed again in clean clothes—clothes into which the smells of the mortuary had not entered, nor the smoky staleness of the room at the police station—after that, he would begin to try to work things out. After that, he would think about what to do next.

But the thoughts would not wait. He dried his face, and ran fingers over it against the beard-grain, and then he looked at his face. He thought, whoever it was must look like me, and for almost the first time in his life tried seriously to decide what he did look like. It had never before seemed particularly important.

He had not ever—at least so far as he could now recall—been particularly self-conscious, and to bother too much over appearance was, if you were a man, to be self-conscious. He had never had to ponder what clothes to wear. Convention decided all but a few small matters, and those of little importance. There were, of course, some areas of latitude—primarily in the choice of neckties. But as a banker, who habitually wore white shirts in the city, the latitude allowed, even there, was slight. One did not wear flamboyant neckties, even if one's taste ran to them (as John's did not) any more than one neglected a bi-weekly haircut.

These things were, John thought, only incidental—and at the moment, since he was wearing only a pair of white shorts, irrelevant. He tried to discover the relevant likeness—the relevancies on which a certain likeness, which logically must exist, was based. He found it very difficult for some time to make any progress, since the face he looked at in the mirror was inevitable—was not, in a real sense, a face. It was merely himself. It was not "like" anything. It was *sui generis*. It was merely the reflection of Me.

Yet it was, as other faces were, made up of features. In this case the features were regular. The nose was straight. The mouth was neither particularly large, nor noticeably small; the lips were sharply enough outlined, but not so sharply outlined that anyone, unprompted, would have thought of it twice; the brown eyes were of only moderate size, neither especially close together nor wide apart. There was no curl in his brown hair, which, now still damp from the shower, was disorderly, but was usually orderly enough.

46

The skin of his face was ruddy, but not red; he looked like a man who spent some time out of doors, but not a great deal —like a man who had not been gravely ill, who had not at any time lacked proper food, nor been under especial nervous strain. He did not look like a man who "drank too much" or one who could, conceivably, be fanatical about anything—including a reasonable amount of drinking. At the moment, there was a faint film of weariness on his face, but only that. If marks were to be left by this thing which was happening, they would appear later, had not yet appeared.

"I look," John Hayward said, and spoke aloud, to the image in the mirror, "like damn' near everybody I know."

He was mildly surprised to discover this, having never before bothered to think about it. Dressed, he thought, I look more like a banker than, say, an advertising man. A banker or a youngish corporation lawyer. Like Richard Still. He thought about Still . . . Still was about his height, about his weight. Still's hair was a little darker; his chin was somewhat more rounded. (Or was it? John rubbed his own chin.) Still was about his age—perhaps a year older. (He had been a year ahead at Harvard.) Oh yes—Dick Still didn't part his hair. (At least, John didn't remember that he did.)

He thought of others—of Al Curtis; of Henry Roberts, who had a desk near his at the bank; of Forrest Carrington (although Carrington was "in" steel); of Russ Norton (although Russ was Princeton); good Lord, he thought—even Pit Woodson.

If, before the self-scrutiny of that afternoon, John Hayward had been told he was a "type" he would, without resentment, have said, sure, he supposed he was. He would have wondered, for a few minutes, why anyone thought the point one worth making, and would then have dismissed the matter from his mind. One was what one was. There were worse ways to be, as certainly it could be argued there were better. Some men (although obviously not many) were destined to be Winston Churchills; others (probably even fewer) Robert

47

Frosts. The majority were more typical, if that was the word one preferred.

John did not, looking into the mirror, finally turning away from it, fight against the realization that, at any rate superficially, he resembled almost everybody he knew. But, for the first time in his life, he did acutely realize it. And it made a starting point. He held to that, pushing away, as well as he could, the swirl of problems which must, eventually, be faced. (What would be the attitude at the bank? What would his father, retired and in Florida, think when the astounding news reached him there? Suspected of murder, does one communicate with friends, pleading innocence? He had a weekend engagement with the Fawcetts in Chappaqua. Should he telephone his apologies, explaining that something (murder) had come up? And there was Barbara—but least of all, yet, could he think of Barbara.)

He dressed. He went into the living room and opened windows, and let the spring air in. Someone who looked like him —that was the starting point. Someone who, standing in a hall with the light behind him, could be mistaken for John Hayward. It was best, provisionally, to presume an honest mistake by the elderly, fat janitor—best to assume that only one man had plotted.

(For an instant, then, without warning, as he stood in the familiarity of the living room, the strange fear swept again through John's mind. If he could remember everything, *would that other living room also be familiar? As familiar as this?* For that instant, darkness seemed to eddy in his mind. John put a hand on the desk by which he was standing, steadying himself in the darkness. The fear passed, but for some seconds a kind of mental emptiness was left behind. Then, again, he was John Hayward, who had lived only one life. The objects of that life were tangible about him.)

He sat down at the desk and opened it. A man who looked as he did, and could write as he did. He reached into a drawer in which he kept his most recently canceled checks. For a moment he groped, and then found the bundle of checks at the back of the drawer, which was not its proper place.

So, John thought—of course they would. They had done it very well; the desk was not disordered; there was no obvious disorder in the apartment. But by the time he had gone through the canceled checks, the searcher had forgotten exactly where in the drawer he had found them.

John took out several of the checks and examined his own signature, as he had examined his own face. He had, at first, much the same difficulty in examining objectively. After he had looked at the signature several times, he managed to see it as a name handwritten—any name. It was a simple signature, firm and legible, lacking in idiosyncrasy. He didn't, John thought, seem to have many idiosyncrasies of any kind. The signature varied somewhat from check to check; it would, John decided, be difficult to prove, even with expert opinion, that the signature on the other checks—those made out to the real estate company—were forged. Experts would, no doubt, be found to differ from one another; they usually could be.

The telephone rang. A newspaper reporter would like a statement; he would like to come around and get an interview. John said a firm "no" to the last request; he considered the first, briefly. He said, "I never saw Miss Evans alive. I know nothing about her death." "Then—" the reporter said. "Period," John said.

The call was the first of several calls, of the same import. John said the same to each. The woman of the *Journal-American* was insistent. She said John ought to give his side; there was an intimation that, if he proved stubborn, he could not blame newspapers for what they printed. "I can sue them," John said, and hung up. He did not know whether this was the way to go about it. He lacked experience. And, he did not want interruptions. After the fifth telephone call, John did not cradle the telephone. He laid it on the desk.

He began to walk restlessly around the room. He felt need, urgent need, for immediate action, but he could not decide what the action should be. He would have to get another lawyer, of course. Perhaps Dick Still could suggest— John shook his head. He would get a lawyer of another type; a type which Dick Still presumably would not suggest. Tomorrow—he would get a lawyer tomorrow.

And, John thought, the lawyer will take the case and do what he can and—he won't believe me. He will listen, and he will nod (because I am paying him) instead of shaking his head, as Miller did, as the others did. But he will think what they thought. Probably he will say, as they said, "You're saying the wrong thing, Mr. Hayward. There's no use saying you didn't know the girl. Why don't we—"

For the first time, now that he was quiet, free to think step by step, in an orderly fashion, John Hayward realized that nobody was going to believe him. That was it—nobody in the world would believe that he had not known Nora Evans, had not rented an apartment for her. That, with premeditation, he had murdered her—some might doubt that. That he had not gone to the apartment that afternoon—some might believe that, in spite of Pedersen, the janitor. (After all, the light had been behind John, not on his face.) That there was another murderer—even that some might believe. But the simple, puzzling truth—that nobody would believe, for the equally simple reason that it was preposterous.

Because, John thought—now sitting in a chair, letting a cigarette go out, staring with blank eyes at a familiar wall—because it means that somebody hated me enough to kill a girl to get at me, in the end to get me killed. Nobody will believe that. I am not the kind of man anyone would hate so much, and so deviously. And then, with a sudden coldness in his mind, he realized something else. I, John Hayward thought, do not believe it either. It is beyond belief.

With that thought, uneasiness returned to his mind, and again it seemed that all that was real—which he *knew* to be real—was dissolving about him, in swirling fantasy. It was like nothing which had ever before happened in his mind—a thing for which nothing in his previous life had in any way prepared him. The very orderliness of his life left him, now, vulnerable to this incomprehensible disorder which had overtaken him. Again, that irrational fear that what could not be believed in could not, finally, be true, fluttered in his mind. But now the fear was formless. Any form it might take would be insupportable.

He stood up, abruptly. Almost physically he shook himself. Harshly, he drove his mind back to the world of logic, of order—drove it out of this fantasy of fear—the fear which was like a swirling of darkness around a horrid thing, a thing too hideous to be looked at.

After a moment—but the passage of time was not of the kind a clock can measure—John was free of the dark fears. This, however, left him with apprehensions at once more tangible and more immediate. He would, he told himself, have to quit imagining horrors. Things were tough enough without that. He'd never seen the girl before. He had never been in the Eleventh Street apartment before. (That, entering it, he had felt it vaguely familiar meant only that he had been often in similar apartments.) Certainly, he had never killed anyone. (As an artillery officer in Korea he had, of course, planned to kill, but that did not enter into it. Also, results had not been certain, or visibly personal.)

What was immediately indicated, John decided, was that he do something. It was evident that there were a good many things, none of them particularly pleasant, which would have to be done. For one thing, he would have to face the people at the bank.

That this could be avoided did not occur to John Hayward. The bank was as much a part of his life as any other part; as much, now, a thing to be brought into some sort of adjustment. He looked at his watch, and found it was just three-thirty. He would go down to the bank and—well, what, absurdly, it came to, tell them he had not killed a girl named Nora Evans. It was a preposterous thing to have to tell Martin Phillips, senior vice president of the Cotton Exchange National Bank.

John went to the hall closet for his hat. (A junior executive

51

does not go hatless to his bank, however un-hatted he may go at other times.) He took the hat off the shelf and was closing the door when he saw, on a hanger, a sports jacket he had never seen before. It was more noticeable than any he owned, or would have thought of choosing. It was pushed to one side of the closet—not by any means hidden, but, equally, not obtrusively in sight.

A little dazedly, John took the jacket off the hanger and looked at it. It was a brown-green tweed, dark but rather boldly patterned. Hardly knowing why he did so, John looked for the maker's name. There was no maker's name. John turned the jacket in his hands. Finally, he put it on. It fitted —not perfectly, but well enough; as well as most sports jackets fitted.

There was a small object in the change pocket in the right-hand pocket. Almost before he touched it, John knew what it would be. It would be a key. It was a key. There was, he realized, no doubt what lock the key would fit. He took the jacket off and looked at it again.

The jacket was meant to be recognizable. Somewhere there was a person—or several people—who would recognize it. That was, clearly, what it was for. How it had got in his hall closet—

But that, too, was obvious. Somebody—this other "John Hayward"—had access to the apartment. That was how he had come by the shirts, and the less identifiable underwear shorts. Since there was nothing to indicate that he had forced a lock, and since there was no convenient fire escape, he had either been let in or had got himself a key. By whom, if the one thing was true, and how, if the other, would have to be found out.

This other "John Hayward" had left the jacket for the police to find. But—there was no indication that they had found it. Yet, they had surely searched the apartment; they could hardly have avoided seeing the jacket. Had they left it, with the key in the pocket, for some reason of their own? Did they, perhaps, hope he would try to dispose of jacket and of key?

It was not clear. John hung the jacket again in the closet. He started out. He went back and took the key out of the jacket pocket. On the way downtown to the bank, in a cab, he put the key with his own on his key chain. Perhaps that was what he was supposed to do; perhaps he was playing into the other's hands. But there was no way of knowing. And he might have a use for the key.

IV

THE MAIN DOORS of the bank were closed, and heavy wire mesh was locked across them. John walked past them to another door, and a uniformed guard looked out at him through the glass. The guard opened the door and said, in a voice so noticeably matter of fact as to be entirely unreal, "Good afternoon, sir." John said, "Afternoon, Barney," and went into the bank, and was conscious that the guard had turned and was looking after him.

John walked, and was conscious that he walked a little stiffly, through the bank's wide concourse, with the tellers' low, ornamentally screened, counters on either side. Few looked up as he walked along the concourse and those who did looked, rather quickly, down again at their work.

He went through the gate which led to the general offices and along a narrow corridor between closely set desks; through another gate into another general office, but one in which the desks were set at a dignified distance from one another, so that there was room for each to have beside it a chair for those who came to confer. One of these desks, in a preferred position, near a window, was John Hayward's. His name was on it. His name was still on it.

Not all the desks in this more rarefied area were occupied, but some were and their possessors looked up. They did not, as the tellers had, look embarrassedly away again; they greeted him with nods, with smiles fixed carefully noncommittal. It was as if they waited introduction to a stranger. Then Henry Roberts got up from a desk near John's and came between desks, his hand held out ahead of him and a smile, which almost reached his eyes, firmly on his familiar face. By the time he reached John, and shook his hand, the smile had grown rigid. But it was still there.

He shook John's hand firmly, and at first without words. John waited for the words.

"Just wanted you to know—" Roberts said, and shook even more firmly the hand he held. "What I mean is—" He let go of John's hand. "Hell," he said, "what can a guy say?"

"I don't know, Hank," John said, and looked at Henry Roberts's eyes. He had, in recent hours, looked into the eyes of a good many people—of policemen, of a man trained in law, of an elevator operator. You could tell more than he had realized from looking at people's eyes. There was a kind of flatness about the eyes of those who did not believe you—and a kind of wariness. That look was in Henry Roberts's eyes. Well, John thought, he had a try at it.

"I never saw this girl before," John said.

"Sure you didn't," Henry Roberts said, but now he gave up the effort to meet John's eyes. "All some damn' fool mistake. Well—" He stopped. He was not equal to this. He doesn't, John thought, know how to get out of this.

"Mr. Phillips still around?" John asked, and saw relief flicker in Roberts's eyes.

"Think he is," Roberts said, and spoke quickly, with relief. "Pretty sure he is. Like me to—"

"No," John said. "I'll just barge in."

"Best way," Roberts said. "Well, good luck." He took hold of John's hand and almost at once released it. "Just wanted you to know—" he said, and stopped again.

"Sure," John said. "I appreciate that, Hank."

He went on between the desks. Heads had been raised from work while he talked to Henry Roberts. Now they were bent over work again. He came to a corridor and went down it to a door near the end. The door had Martin Phillips's name on it. John opened the door and went in, and Miriam Lacey looked up at him. She had blue eyes, which grew wide. It was surprising how much one could tell from eyes.

"Oh—Mr. Hayward," she said. "I—"

"Forget it, Miriam," John said. "Is he?" He indicated, with a movement of his head, the private office beyond.

56

"Oh," she said, "I'm afraid somebody's with him." It was evident she was embarrassed. "That is, someone from—"

The door to the private office opened. The man who came out of it was familiar.

"Hello, Mr. Hayward," Detective Grady said. He was quite affable. "Keep running into each other, don't we?"

John nodded.

"Way things are," Grady said. "Well—'afternoon, Miss Lacey."

He went out, then. He had left the door to the private office open.

"Come in, Hayward," Martin Phillips said.

John went in.

Martin Phillips was sixty-one. He had gray hair, thick, smoothly brushed; he was a big man, sitting broad-shouldered behind a spreading desk. He wore a dark gray suit; he held nose-glasses in his left hand and watched John cross a dozen feet of carpeted floor in the big corner office. The light from the corner window was on John's face.

"Sit down, Hayward," Phillips said; and waited while John sat down. "This is bad business," Phillips said.

Phillips had gray eyes. They were noticeably without expression, at least during banking hours. They were without expression now.

"Yes," John said, "it's a very bad business, sir."

"They tell me," Phillips said, "that you deny even knowing this—this girl."

"Nora Evans," John said. "Yes, I do deny that, Mr. Phillips."

"Yes," Phillips said. "And, that you seem to have rented an apartment for her. Paying by check on the Riverside."

"And that I left shirts in the apartment," John said. "And that the janitor identified me. Apparently Grady has—" He hesitated. "Filled you in, sir," he said.

"It seems," Phillips said, "that the police think you are making an error in judgment, Hayward. By this complete denial. It seems to puzzle them."

"Yes," John said.

"And I suppose," Phillips said, "that now you want to know where you stand. With the bank."

It did not appear that he expected an answer.

"This detective," he said, "had the same question. Among others, of course. I told him that your reputation here was good. That we would find it difficult to believe you would be involved in—anything of this nature."

"Well," John said, "thank you, sir."

And he looked into Phillips's expressionless gray eyes. The eyes did not evade his; they were not, as Roberts's had been, embarrassed eyes.

"I do find it difficult to believe," Phillips said. "But—can you explain the circumstances, Hayward?"

"Somebody has framed me," John said. "Arranged these things."

There was no expression in Martin Phillips's eyes. He nodded his head slowly, but there was no acceptance in the movement; it was not affirmative; it indicated words heard and recorded.

"Why?" he said.

"I don't know," John said. He paused. "I realize," he said, "that it isn't easy to believe."

"No," Phillips said. "It isn't a likely story. Our position is difficult, Hayward."

"So is mine," John said. "Rather the more difficult of the two."

"Yes. In any event, you're still an employee of the Cotton Exchange. I told the detective that." John waited. "On leave, of course. With full compensation, of course."

"In other words," John said, "you bide your time."

Phillips raised his heavy eyebrows slightly. He said, "If you want to put it that way."

It had been a lapse from formality, from the proper ordering of words.

"I'm sorry," John said. But he did not feel particularly sorry. "I should have said, 'You reserve judgment.'"

"Don't," Phillips said, "think I am unsympathetic. Under other circumstances—" He did not finish. "You have the Thayer matter in hand," he said. "And—the Tushingham Trust, isn't it?" He waited for John to nod his head. "You might," he said, "bring Roberts up to date on them."

"Yes," John said, and stood up. There hadn't been any miracle. There hadn't been anything.

"You'll want a lawyer," Phillips said. "Or, have you one?"

"A man named Still," John said. "Richard Still. However, he doesn't feel it's his kind of case."

Martin Phillips heard him.

"It would be preferable," he said, "if the bank's firm were not involved. You agree to that?"

"Yes," John said. "I understand, sir. I—is there anything else?"

For some seconds, Phillips looked at him from impervious gray eyes.

"One thing, John," he said, and the use of given name was warning. "About Barbara. I'm afraid that her name can hardly avoid being brought in. From what Detective Grady let drop. But—can I rely on you not to involve her further? In any way?" He stood up behind the desk. "You understand what I mean?"

"Yes," John said. "Quite clearly. Stay away from her." His eyes met those of the older man. "Did you think I'd drag her into a thing like this?" he asked.

"It is hard to know what to think," Phillips said. "There are a good many considerations."

"Yes," John said, "there are, Mr. Phillips."

Then he turned and went out. He spent half an hour bringing Roberts up to date. He felt, as he talked, sitting in the chair at the end of Roberts's desk, that many eyes were on him. The world was very full of eyes—of unbelieving eyes. For an instant, John felt they were all around him, that he was ringed by eyes which were flat with disbelief.

He went out through the office where there was just room to walk, carefully, between many desks, and through the pub-

59

lic concourse. Few of the tellers were in their cages. They would be checking in, balancing out, for the night.

Barney opened the employees' door and said, "Good night, Mr. Hayward," and closed the door after him.

The Phillips Cadillac was parked a few feet down the street. Clay, in uniform, was at the wheel. Barbara was in the back of the car, in the corner farthest from the curb. He thought she slid across the seat, but he turned and walked away from the car, as if he had not seen her. He had agreed to that.

And, he did not want to see what was in Barbara Phillips's eyes.

He walked to the corner and turned into Williams Street. He went the way the crowd was going. At the newsstand by the subway kiosk he bought a copy of the *World-Telegram and Sun.* He started into the subway and changed his mind, and bucked his way out again and, after a little waiting, got a cab. In the cab, he read the *World-Telegram and Sun,* the paper jiggling in front of his eyes.

There was a three-column picture on the front page and under it a picture of John Hayward, smaller than the other, and, balancing that, a photograph of the outside of the apartment house on Eleventh Street. The photograph of John had been taken as he left the courtroom, and he looked, he thought, more than ever like everyone else. But the three-column picture was not a photograph. It was the reproduction of a drawing. The drawing was of Nora Evans. Above the picture were the words: "Murdered Girl: Who Was She?" and below, "'Nora Evans,' mystery victim of Village murder."

John read the news story then, in the joggling cab, the print jumping before his eyes.

"Police investigating the strangulation murder Saturday of 'Nora Evans,' whose almost nude body was found in her Greenwich Village apartment by a cleaning woman, concentrated today on an effort to trace the girl's background, about which they have so far been able to discover little," John read.

"It is probable, the police say, that the name by which she was known was assumed to disguise her real identity.

"Meanwhile, John Hayward, of —— East Thirty-sixth Street, an executive of the Cotton Exchange Bank, was arraigned as a material witness in the case before Magistrate Silverman in Felony Court and released in $20,000 bail. The police assert that Mr. Hayward, a Harvard graduate and assistant to the bank's senior vice president, Martin Phillips, was an associate of the murdered girl.

"In response to questions, Mr. Hayward denied categorically that he had known 'Miss Evans' or visited her apartment in East Eleventh Street. The police allege that the rent of the apartment was paid by a man, whom they refuse to identify."

The implication, John realized, was obvious—and only an implication. There was no statement that John Hayward was the man the police refused to identify. One was hardly needed. John read on. The account reverted to the "mystery" of Nora Evans's identity.

She had—if one could trust what the police told the press, which was perhaps not everything—appeared out of nowhere the October before, when she had first looked at the apartment. On her second visit, which ended with her agreement to rent the apartment, she had been accompanied by a man. She had moved in a few weeks later. Furniture had been delivered, new, from one of the city's largest (and most expensive) stores. Police investigation had disclosed that the furniture had been purchased a few days before its delivery and had been paid for in cash. A salesman—who had been politely astonished at his own good fortune—remembered the pretty red-haired girl very well. He remembered the cash very well. And the only address she had given had been the Eleventh Street address.

Since each apartment there had its own lock-box for mail, there was no way of knowing what mail the girl had received during the months she lived there. There had been some, not many, deliveries from specialty shops. She had bought gro-

61

ceries, sparingly, from a neighborhood store; she had bought
liquor, also in small quantities, from another. She had paid in
cash for both food and drink. The cost of electricity and gas
had been included in the rent; she had paid the telephone
bills in cash. The telephone company records showed no
charges for out-of-town calls. There was no indication that
she had had a bank account.

And, so far, the police had found no picture of the dead
girl in her apartment. They had been unable to locate anyone who "admitted" knowing her. (The word was, evidently,
chosen as a reference word. The reference was to John Hayward, whom the police would not identify as the renter of
"Miss Evans's" apartment.)

"Somewhere," the reporter wrote, "a pretty girl with red
hair grew up. Somewhere she went to school—made friends,
no doubt went on dates with boy friends. Somewhere, before
October, she lived—alone? sharing an apartment with another
girl? perhaps with her husband? None of these questions can
the police answer.

"Medical evidence fixes her age as in the middle or early
twenties. The color of her hair was its natural color. The
Medical Examiner's report describes her as 'well nourished.'
Her nails were manicured; most of her clothing was of good
quality, and much of it expensive.

"Was she employed, as an office worker or perhaps as a
model? The police have been able to find no social security
card. She did not own a car, or if she did the registration
certificate has not been unearthed. She was not licensed to
operate a car. At least, no operator's permit has been found.
She had no charge accounts. If she received mail, she de-
stroyed it after she had read it. The only key found among
her effects was that to the apartment in which she lived and
died.

"Somehow, for some reason, the girl known as 'Nora Evans'
stepped from a background which can only be guessed at
into a new life, almost certainly with a new, but shadowy,
identity, when, last November, she moved into a charming,

newly-furnished, apartment in one of Greenwich Village's better neighborhoods."

The reporter paused there, presumably to regain his breath. He went on, more prosaically:

"The drawing reproduced in the *World-Telegram and Sun* was made by a police artist, after the girl's death. The police hope it will be identified by someone who may have known 'Miss Evans' in the past."

"Here we are," the cab driver said.

John paid him, and got out, carrying the newspaper.

"Hell of a thing," the driver said. "Pretty girl like that. What would anybody want to kill a girl like that for?"

"I don't know," John said, and went into his apartment house. I don't know, he thought, riding up in the elevator. *I don't know.* He went into his apartment, which seemed emptier than he had ever known it—which seemed somehow strange—and put his hat on the closet shelf. He looked at the too-emphatic sports jacket on its hanger.

Slowly, very carefully, he closed the closet door. He went, quite methodically, to the refrigerator and to his liquor cabinet, and made himself a drink. He felt only deep weariness.

Instead of coming clear, he thought (standing as he sipped his drink) all of it was slipping into greater obscurity. Now there were two areas obscured, where there had been before only one—who had impersonated him to murder? Now there was this entirely unexpected question—who had been murdered?

"We get nowhere fast," John Hayward said, prosaically and aloud, to hear the sound of his own voice, to reduce things to simple, ordinary words. And he thought, then, it's too much to try alone. He thought of Barbara, and forced his thoughts from her, so that there was only an emptiness where she had been.

V

BARBARA PHILLIPS SAID, "Never mind, Clay," and reached the width of the car seat to open the door for her father. Martin Phillips said, "Good evening, Barbara," without surprise. Nor was he surprised when, the door closed, his daughter leaned forward, in that quick, fluid way of hers, and rolled up the glass which separated them from the chauffeur. He sighed, faintly, but he was not surprised.

Barbara heard the sigh. Briefly, she patted his nearest hand, as an act of comradeship. But then, as the car started, she leaned back in her corner and looked at him. She looked at him from widely spaced brown eyes, set in a pointed face. She's the prettiest thing there ever was, her father thought and said, smiling a little, "Well, Barbara?"

"John was in there," she said, moving her close-cropped head a little toward the bank building. "I saw him when he came out. He very carefully didn't see me." She paused. Her father nodded his banker's head. "It won't do you any good, darling," she said. "Not any good at all." She waited. But he waited too, smiling faintly—in comradeship—but, she realized, letting her set the pace. He's a very intelligent man, my father, she thought.

"Because," she said, "I won't have it. You've worked on John. Appealed to his ethical sense. Oh, I know you both. It's—it's something out of the dim past."

"What is?" Martin Phillips permitted himself to say, and was told there was no sense in pretending.

"I," she said, "am to be shielded. To be kept above the battle. Look at me."

He did.

"You," she said, "should know better. You should know me better. I don't expect him to, yet. Men have funny ideas about their women, particularly at first. Women—let them."

His face changed a great deal, when he really smiled. He said, "Thanks for telling me, Barbara," and then, but very briefly, a smile widened her delicately cut, but entirely ample, mouth. I've always been glad, Martin Phillips thought, that she hasn't got a little rosebud mouth. She is very like her mother was. Only—quicker. "So, you're Hayward's woman, are you?"

"Yes," she said. "Entirely. More than he knows—or needs to know."

"Although," her father said, "you're really a child. Twenty-three next September."

Her gesture dismissed that.

"Then," he said, "your man's in a bad spot, Barbara. Do you know how bad a spot?"

"I've read the papers," she said.

"Worse than that," he said. "Considerably worse. The police came to see me, too. Listen—" He told her how bad a spot John Hayward was in. He told it with economy, dispassionately. He watched her dark eyes; could feel her quick mind ordering what he told her. He watched for doubt to grow in her eyes. It did not.

"And with all that," she said. "You—you what? Told him the bank would reserve judgment? That you would? And—that you trusted him not to bring me into so—so squalid—a situation?"

But there was no reproach in her tone.

"Yes," he said. "That's approximately what I told Hayward."

"Taking advantage," she said, "of being his boss. Taking advantage of the dignity of the bank. Taking advantage of being my father."

"Yes," he said. "Taking any advantage I could, my dear."

"And of course," she said, "the poor baby was—taken in. You knew he would be, because he's that kind of person. You counted on that."

"Yes," Martin Phillips said.

"Knowing that," she said. "Knowing the kind he is, you

66

could still believe—or even half believe—he would kill a girl he'd—" She hesitated, seeking a term her father would not, on her lips, find inappropriate. "Been making love to?" she said.

She is considerate of the conservatism of age, her father thought. It's a long time between generations. She's a very nice girl. He was sorry for her; sorrier than she would want him to show.

"My dear," he said, "there are a good many things you don't know about. Ugly things—violent things."

"Are there?" she said.

"I," Martin Phillips said, "would certainly prefer to think so. As to John—I've always thought very highly of his character. And, for that matter, of his intelligence. But—"

"You consider the evidence," she said. "What on earth has the evidence to do with it? And—thinking he may be a murderer, because of all this evidence—you put him on his honor." She looked intently at her father. "I suppose," she said, "you didn't really use that word?"

That word out of antiquity, Martin Phillips thought. "No," he said. "I spared him that, Barbara." He reached out, petted her knee. "It's a shocking thing," he said. "I—I love you very much, my dear. I—"

She put a slender hand on his large hand.

"Oh," she said. "I know. There's no blame." She patted his hand; sat back in the corner of the seat. "I've been trying to get him on the telephone," she said. "I'm going to keep on trying." She waited. She said, "You hear me, father?"

"Yes," he said.

"Can't you understand what's happening to him?" she said, and for the first time her voice, so desperately kept matter of fact, faltered. "Can't you—" Then she put both hands over her eyes, and her body trembled. "What kind of person do you think I am?" she said. "What kind of—of wax doll—do you think you have for a daughter?" Her clear voice, her very young voice, was smudged. She took her hands down from her face. "Look at me," she said. "You—you loved mother. Can't you see I love John? Can't you—remember?"

"Yes," he said. "I remember, Barbara. But—you seem so young." He hesitated. "It's possible," he said, "to fall in love with the wrong people. Not to know what kind of people they are. As you get older—" He stopped himself; the young are easily alienated from the old. He decided that, perhaps fortunately, she was not really listening.

"He must," Barbara said, "think I'm like all the rest. That —that all the facts in the world would make any difference."

He did not try to answer that. I don't, he thought, really know the answer to that. All I know is, you have to act as if facts do make a difference, because there isn't any other way to act. Not, he thought, as you get older.

The car had been going up Park Avenue. It turned to the right off Park. Clay found a place to bring it to the curb. Clay did not, as under other circumstances he would have, get out and come around to open the door. He thought they might not have finished. He supposed it was about Mr. Hayward who had killed what appeared to be a damn' good-looking girl. It was tough on Miss Barbara.

"I'll keep at it until I get him," Barbara said. "I'll make him let me help. However much he tries—" She did not finish.

"Yes," her father said, "I suppose you will, Barbara. I don't suppose I can stop you."

She patted his hand again.

"In most respects," she said, "you're a very satisfactory father."

"As fathers go," Martin Phillips said, and got out of the car and held his hand out to her, who needed no help, who came out of the car as light as a floating feather. How heavy the years make us, her father thought—how weighted down with facts.

* * *

John Hayward paid the cab driver and crossed the sidewalk of Forty-fourth Street and went into the Harvard Club.

68

He found the distance from the cab to club lobby far longer than he had ever known it to be; although he went quickly enough, his mind held back. Inside, he felt that he walked stiffly, conscious of inimical eyes. Actually, he encountered, on his way to the bar, only Pit Woodson, on patrol, as always, for bridge players. And Pit's face—the regular-featured, well-cared-for face of his type, and John's—lighted up and he came forward, with a hand out. "Johnny boy," Pit said. "*Good* to see you."

John said, "'Lo, Pit," and took the hand offered him. It appeared, at first, that the news had not penetrated to Pit Woodson. But then, looking more carefully into Pit Woodson's slightly prominent brown eyes, he perceived there a flicker which he took to be of wariness. So Pit had heard. The news had permeated to the most remote bridge table. Which was to be expected; which John had expected.

"Hows about—" Pit Woodson began, the flicker no longer in his eyes—in his eyes only the warm friendliness of a bridge player in search of three others.

"Sorry, Pit," John said. "Afraid I'm tied up." He said this almost by instinct. Probably, he thought, he had said much the same thing Saturday afternoon. (And yet, when one felt like bridge, there was no man in the club, or anywhere else John could think of, better at it than Pit Woodson. The trouble was, presumably, that few felt quite so much like quite so much bridge as Pit did.) "Another time," John said and Pit Woodson said, "Sure, any time," which could be taken literally.

John went into the bar still feeling a kind of stiffness, a consciousness of inimical eyes all about him. Al Curtis was alone near an end of the bar, as he had promised he would be—promised cheerfully enough, after only a momentary pause—when John had got him on the telephone. He had, to be sure, and after that first momentary hesitation, suggested another meeting place. It had been John who had said that he'd much rather they made it the club, and had added he would explain later.

Because, John had decided, in the emptiness of his apartment, what had happened at the club on Saturday afternoon was the simplest, and the most immediate, place to start. The police had been right on that; they had, unfortunately, seemed to be right about almost everything. Whoever had laid the trap had needed to know one thing: that, at between three and four o'clock Saturday afternoon, John could not prove his whereabouts. And that knowledge probably had been gained at the club.

(It was conceivable, of course, that the murderer had merely chanced to see John sauntering along Fifth Avenue, window shopping at jewelers, and had moved quickly, the trap being ready and only its springing to be done. But this would have been leaving much to chance, and it appeared that, in other respects, the murderer had left little.)

"Hi, John," Al Curtis said, and he made no pretense that he did not know. He went so far as to pat John's shoulder while, briefly, they waited for drinks. But the good-fellowship of that was only formal; Curtis's face remained without expression, there was constraint in his eyes. (Standing side by side at the bar, John thought, we are almost precisely of a height. Perhaps Al is a few pounds heavier. His eyes are gray and his hair is lighter than mine.)

By agreement, unspoken, they took their drinks to a table. On the way they passed a larger table, at which half a dozen men sat—older men, known to John only as members he had seen before, usually in the bar. But one of the men looked up as they passed and then, as a result, presumably, of some comment softly made, the others looked. They looked carefully at John Hayward, and it seemed to him that all their eyes narrowed; that suspicion, even a kind of resentment, emanated from the eyes of the men at the table. He felt the muscles of his neck stiffen again, and he looked away from the men at the table.

"I'm in a hell of a spot," John said, when they were seated.

"Yes," Curtis said. "So I gather. Anything I can—" But he

70

did not finish, and his tone was detached, committed him to even less than the half-made offer.

"There might be," John said. "They've got me mixed up with someone else."

Al Curtis nodded to that, but he said nothing. John told him how things stood, or told him enough. A good deal depended, obviously, on Saturday afternoon.

"When the girl was killed," Curtis said. "Yes, I should think it might."

John felt his nerves tighten at the tone. But he could not let them.

"It was deliberate," he said. "It was planned the way it's working out. So, there was one thing somebody had to know." He told Al Curtis what it was.

"In short," Curtis said, "did you tell me that you were going to take this—walk?" His eyes narrowed. "You're not getting ideas, are you? About me?"

"I'm trying to get things straight," John said. "I haven't got any ideas about anybody. You see—" He paused. "Look," he said, "I want you to help me piece it out. It didn't have any importance then. Sometimes, things like that—unimportant things—two people can remember. Maybe something somebody said will remind one of—"

"All right," Curtis said. "I know what you mean. All right —as I remember it, you said something like that. Yes."

"We came out of the dining room," John said. "Started toward the door and you said something—wait a minute. You'd started on ahead—"

"Yeah," Curtis said. "I turned around and said something about, could I drop you somewhere. You said no because—" He shrugged. "Hell," he said, "it was pretty damn' trivial. How d'you expect anybody—"

"Wait," John said, "wasn't it this way? Didn't you say you'd drop me and didn't I say something about doing some shopping? Or—first that I thought I'd walk home and then, that maybe I'd do a little shopping on the way?"

71

"I guess it was something like that," Curtis said. He watched John.

But now it had come back; most of it had come back.

They had still been inside; there had been several other men within earshot, drifting from a leisurely lunch toward the street, toward a leisurely afternoon. (Toward bars, toward girls, toward homes and wives.)

"I said I guessed not," John said. "That I thought I'd give my legs a stretch. That I had one or two things I wanted to pick up. Don't you remember that?"

"It sounds right," Curtis said. "I remember you came out about the same time I did, and I got a cab and—yeah, I remember you were walking up toward Fifth."

"Pit Woodson," John said, "there were several around. He was one of them. But—did I say anything to him about having a date?"

"Don't remember you did," Curtis said, but then he shrugged slightly. "But it is something one says to Pit. Good old Pit."

"Who else?" John said. "You remember anybody else?"

"No," Al Curtis said, but then he said, "Wait a minute. Dick Still was around. Maybe he was the one told Pit he had a date. And your pal Roberts. Wasn't he around?"

"Hank Roberts? No, I don't think—"

"Sure he was," Curtis said. "Just coming in from the bar. You'd have had your back to him, probably. He had somebody with him—Princeton man. Named—hell, I met him. Morton or something."

"Russ Norton? Was that who it was?"

It sounded right, Curtis said. Anything special about a Russ Norton?

"Friend of a friend of mine," John said. "No, nothing special."

(A man who, a year or so ago, had seen a good deal of Barbara Phillips. Had taken her places and—)

"Hank Roberts," John said. "Dick Still. Pit—looking for a fourth."

"Probably," Curtis said, "for a second and a third, too."

"This man who was maybe Russ Norton. Anybody else you remember?"

"Who could have heard you? Two or three others, I'd think. And—I heard you, I was the one you were talking to."

"All right," John said, "where did you go, Al? When you drove off in a cab?"

Curtis looked at him for some time.

"It's none of your business, is it?" Curtis said, finally. "But —I went to see a girl friend. I had a very pleasant afternoon. And—she doesn't live in the Village. And she hasn't got red hair. And, oh yes, she's still alive." He looked at John again, from expressionless eyes. "Very, very much alive," Al Curtis said. "If you know what I mean, Hayward."

There was enmity in Curtis's voice and to it, John realized, he had no answer, could make no apology. It was only for himself, John thought, that the order of things had broken down, and with it the established reticencies. To Al Curtis, what one did, and whom one saw were matters not to be enquired into by outsiders; for him, that had not changed. Intrusion—particularly when it might be interpreted to involve suspicion—was still something to be surprised at, and to resent.

And yet, John thought—sipping his drink, not directly answering—I don't know it is only that. I don't, actually, know Al Curtis. I only know about him—that he is my age or near enough, and went to Harvard; that he has a place in the country with a tennis court, and that he knows a good many of the people I know. But when you come to it, John thought further—lighting a cigarette—I don't know them, either. They are merely familiar—familiar shapes and faces, familiar voices, familiar opinions and habits. Pit Woodson lives for bridge, but I don't know why. Hank Roberts is a Democrat, and I don't know why. Russ Norton—

"Well?" Curtis said, from across the table.

"Oh," John said. "Sorry, Al."

73

"It's all right," Al Curtis said. "Only, don't get ideas. Ready for another?"

John wasn't. But he was about to say he was, so to make conventional amends, when a club servant came through the bar, looking from table to table. He found what he sought, as John had, suddenly, known he would, and came to their table and said, "Telephone, Mr. Hayward."

John stood up at once and said, "Thanks, Al," and followed the servant. He went into a booth and said, "This is John Hayward."

"The signals you and Dad worked out," Barbara Phillips said. "They're off. I'm a girl won't be protected."

He could not answer for a moment. Her voice was too clear, came too clearly from a remembered hour.

"So," Barbara said, seeming entirely to understand his silence, "you buy me a drink, and dinner and then we go to work on this. Together."

"No," he said. "It's bad enough for you already."

"Oh," she said, "don't you know anything? *Not anything?*" Although she did not raise her voice, there was a cry in it. But at the same time there was, evidently, irritation. "Don't you see I can't be left out? Won't be left out?"

"Your father was right," he said. "Don't think I—"

"There's no right or wrong about it," she said, not waiting. "To him, I'm a daughter. He can't help that. To you, I'm—whatever you want to call it. I don't know what you do call it. But to me, I'm me. Where will you meet me?"

"I promised your father—" he said.

"You're unpromised, then. I'm at the Algonquin. There? Or, shall I come and picket the Harvard Club?"

In spite of everything, he smiled at that. She was here, there and everywhere, and lovely. And, as the smile faded, it was because a moment of tender amusement was submerged, engulfed, by his great longing to see her, to hear her voice close, not thus strained through mechanism.

"And," she said, "I told my father. He's wiser than you. A little. He knows, now, that it won't work." She paused, for an

74

instant. "And before you say it," she said, "I won't have you stuffy. Standing on ethics. Where?"

It was no good. He had known it would be no good. Something sang in his mind because it would be no good.

"Not the Algonquin," he said. He had been there only once or twice; he thought it would be full of gossip columnists, of writers—probably of people who wrote for newspapers. She, at any rate, they would recognize; perhaps from his picture, they would recognize him. (Although I look like everybody.) He could avoid that, or try to. He said, "It shouldn't be anywhere. I know that, if you don't. But—you know Monet's?" It was a small place in the East Fifties, near Third. It had a tiny, uncrowded lounge—uncrowded, at any rate, until later.

She knew Monet's.

"I'll meet you there," he said. "In the bar. In about half an hour."

"Why you don't merely walk down the street—" she began, but then said, "Oh, all right. Perhaps you're right."

He left the booth. At a table near it, Pit Woodson had assembled his second and his third and his fourth. "Four no trump," Pit said. He was quite changed at the bridge table, particularly when in pursuit of a slam. Hank Roberts was Pit's partner. He said, "Five hearts." It appeared that they might be on their way, although Roberts was by no means as good as Pit.

John went out into the late light of Forty-fourth Street. Across the street, doing nothing in particular, was a tall man with a drooping face. This was unanticipated. But, thought about, it was, of course, something to be expected. On bail or not on bail, he was also on a string. Detective Nathan Shapiro, of the sad eyes, was part of the string.

It was instinct, or seemed to be, that sent John's hand up in signal to an approaching cab. It was luck the cab was empty.

It was not rational—or could be rationalized only as an effort, still, to keep Barbara out of it. Why, he wondered, even as he said, "Grand Central" to the cab driver, am I doing this? This is a kind of running. I've—well, paid my dues. For the time being. But then he realized why. It was not impossible that that particular segment of time had run out; that Shapiro was on hand to pick him up.

Well, he would see Barbara first, however he ran for it—whatever it looked like to Shapiro and Miller and the rest. At any rate, he'd try.

He looked back, through the rear glass. He could not see Shapiro. But it was unlikely that Shapiro would be easily shaken off, if he wanted to stay on. Probably he had a car ready, or a cab.

John's own cab stopped for the lights at Fifth. It stopped again at Madison; at Vanderbilt, a traffic patrolman held up his hand against the cab. Shapiro wouldn't need transport; he could keep up on foot. Finally, they stopped in the station's cab port.

John went down the stairs, by no means running—going no faster than a man might with a train to catch. At the bottom of the stairs, he turned sharply right and then, after he had passed Schrafft's food shop, left. He went through a narrow door, down steep stairs, to the bar-restaurant. But he did not actually go into it. He went left into the corridor outside the men's room on the lower level. He went through and came out on the lower level.

He walked through the concourse, not hurrying now; now stopping to take a timetable from a rack, and so making an opportunity to look back. He saw a good many people, but not Shapiro. It was possible that he had been shaken off. (It was also possible that he had not really intended to stay on. It was conceivable that he had had other business across the street from the Harvard Club. John had no knowledge as to how many irons a policeman might keep simultaneously in the fire.)

John went through the lower level concourse, and through a passage to the East Side subway. The rush hour had waned, but the platforms still were crowded. He walked the length of one platform, through the crowd, and up the stairs and

76

back to the street again. He bought a newspaper at a stand, and took time to look about. There was no sign of Shapiro. He got a cab, after a little waiting on the corner, and was driven to Monet's.

It had not really taken half an hour, but she was there. She was at a table in a corner of the small room, and the corner would have been dark if she had not been there.

For a moment she did not seem to see him, and in that moment, John felt again that peculiar coldness in his mind. What would he see when he looked into her eyes? In spite of all she said, what would her eyes betray? For eyes betray; he knew that now. It was one of the things he had learned since, less than forty-eight hours ago, he had seen her last.

John walked through the dim room toward the light in the corner.

She saw him, then. As he came toward her, she held out both hands across the table. For a moment he stood looking down at her, looking into her dark eyes. Although she smiled, there was sadness in her eyes. But there was no doubt in them.

It is not difficult to believe when you are not alone.

John leaned down to her and, for an instant, her lips seemed to leap under his.

He sat down, then, opposite her.

"For one who's not the public kissing type," Barbara Phillips said, and it was as easy as that—as casual seeming as that, and as close as that. "We can do with a drink," she said and then, absurdly, her voice trembled a little. Of all the absurd things, Barbara Phillips thought. I do all right and then I ask for a drink and then—*then* of all times. "Can I," she said, quite steadily, "have a whiskey sour?"

"I don't approve," John said. "But—yes."

It was as easy as that, again. Their drinks came, and she started to drink a little rapidly, and stopped herself. He was watching her across the table. He looks older than he did, she thought. But his face hasn't changed.

"Was it awful?" she said. "Tell me, darling."

77

She used the word "darling" often, as many do. She did not often use the word in this special way.

He told her. It took considerable time. It took another drink, and when, upstairs, in a booth, they had finished dinner, it still was not all told.

Finally it was.

"Who was the girl?" she said, and for an instant the question startled him. She saw the surprise in his eyes, patted his nearer hand, told him not to be an idiot. "You think it's against *you*," she said. "Perhaps it is. But—why? And—why not against the girl?"

He shook his head.

"The police wonder that," she said. "And—need to know. That must be why they did it this way—let you go, as a witness. Instead of keeping you in jail. Isn't that true? Because there's a gap in what they know?"

"Probably," he said.

"John," she said, "why did you keep the key?"

He was not entirely clear, he told her. He'd thought that, somehow, he might use it. Then he said, "That picture of me. If I knew where it was taken, it might—" He spread his hands a little. "It won't be there now," he said.

"When I was quite a small girl," Barbara Phillips said, "my father had a saying. 'You never know till you try,' he used to say. A good many people say that, I suppose. Father is usually more original. Still—"

"Not you," John said, but there was no conviction in his voice.

"I," Barbara said, "am a girl won't be protected. I thought we were clear on that."

VI

IT HAD GROWN dark when they left the restaurant. But complete darkness is not permitted on Manhattan's streets. There was light enough, as they waited for a cab, for John to look around—look first across the street, and then to right and to left. He did not see Shapiro, or any of the others. But, to his right, a man was standing looking into a lighted show window. John wondered what engrossed him, and thought that New York has many detectives. But then a cab came.

If they wanted him, they would get him, later if not now —at his apartment if not on the streets.

"Was that the man?" she said. "Shapiro?"

"No," he said. "Nobody I ever saw before."

She came close to him in the cab, and he held her close.

"I'll have to see your father," he said. "Tell him I—couldn't go through with it."

"Men," she said. "If it makes you happy. When you take me home—afterward."

The cab went downtown, down Park and Fourth. The traffic had thinned; the cab rolled fast. From Broadway they went through Eleventh, across University Place. The cab driver said, "Here you are," and knocked up the meter flag. He was paid, and drove away.

"Wait," Barbara said. "I'll look for that friend of mine. Her name's Hilda Zook. The poor thing."

They had arranged that, John, at first reluctantly. She would look at mailboxes, seeking the name of a friend—a friend, as it turned out, improbably named Zook. And seeing who there was to see. He had protested. She had said, "Nonsense. It's the most innocent-seeming thing in the world."

He waited only briefly. She reappeared at the apartment house door and nodded. The small lobby was empty; neither the janitor Pedersen nor policemen lurked there. Upstairs might well be different. They went up in the automatic elevator. In the corridor upstairs no one waited.

The key from the pocket of the too-loud jacket fitted. It had been inevitable that it would fit; otherwise, it was meaningless, part of no pattern. That there be a pattern was essential. John pushed the door open and reached for the light switch, and two lamps in the sunken living room went on. Then he stopped, and looked at his hand, still raised.

"I knew where it was," he said slowly, and to his own ears his voice seemed to come from far off.

"What?" Barbara said. "Oh—oh for heaven's sake, John." She took both his arms in her hands, faced him. "You're too big to shake," she said. Her eyes were very bright. "You're an idiot." She released his arms. "Where else would it be?" she said. "They're always there."

He looked down at her.

"You know, then?" he said.

"That you've had a bad time," she said. "That you have more imagination than's good for you. The last I've known for months."

"That I—" he said, and stopped in bewilderment. "I?"

"Who else?" she said. "There are hundreds of apartments like this one. Light switches are always in pretty much the same place. Where else?" She stopped for a moment. "We're wasting time," she said. "Have they taken the picture?"

From the raised entrance platform, John could not tell. They went down into the living room. The photograph was where it had been, on a small table. The daffodils were no longer there.

They looked at the photograph. "You were playing tennis," she said. "Had been, or were going to. I'd guess, going to."

The background was out of focus. There was the faint tracing of what might be the wire netting of a backstop. Beyond that, there was, even more faintly, part of a tree—apparently a big tree, fully in leaf. The surface of the court was not visible; the photograph showed John's body only above the waist.

There was not much to go on. Some place in the country,

since only in the country, recently, had he played tennis; somewhere with a tree near the court. He had, the summer before, played as a guest at several clubs—in Westchester, on Long Island. He had played on Al Curtis's private court, with Al and two other men, whom he had known by given names, for a few hours and now did not remember. He had played—

She couldn't help with that, Barbara thought. In another way she might. What kind of girl was the girl who had lived here, who had died here? What kind of clothes had she worn? What scent had she used?

Barbara left John standing by the little table, looking at the photograph. He was so intent—intent in his effort to recapture memory—that he did not, she thought, know that she had left, had walked across the living room and into the bedroom. She found a light switch there and flicked it up, and lamps went on on a dressing table. At what she saw, Barbara Phillips for a moment raised a surprised hand to her lips.

There were twin beds in the room, and on one of them clothing was piled—had, apparently, been thrown. Woolen dresses and cotton dresses and silk dresses; a silk suit and a woolen suit; two evening dresses, one of them long; a very pretty, very fragile, negligee—all piled helter-skelter on the bed.

For a moment, Barbara's chief feeling was one of regret that pretty things should be so treated—it was a feeling, almost, of sympathy for the pretty things. But then she went from the doorway to the bed and began to pick up the garments, one by one—the negligee, the short evening dress. The girl had been size ten; she had had good taste. And, she had had money to spend.

Without thinking, acting almost instinctively, Barbara looked for the shop's label in the evening dress she held. Fifth Avenue it would be, almost certainly—or Madison, or Fifty-seventh Street.

There was no label.

This did not, of course, mean anything. Labels are lightly sewed on; not infrequently, they fall off. (To a coat, a girl would sew a label back, if it was the label of a good shop. On an evening dress, or a negligee, a girl probably would not bother.) Still idly, Barbara picked up one of the woolen dresses and again looked for the label. And, again, there was no label.

But this time, she took the dress across the room to the light, and held it under the light and bent over it. The label had not merely pulled loose. It had been cut out. Cut ends of thread were evident.

She worked quickly, then. Garment by garment she went over the pretty things on the bed, laying them aside more neatly, more tenderly, than they had been laid. Before she had gone far, she realized what she would discover—that from each of the things which had hung in the girl's closet, the label had been cut. Probably, Barbara thought, with a pair of manicure scissors.

Except for one—a sheath of wool, dark green. From that, she was almost certain, the label had not been neatly cut. An end of thread hung loose. That label had been pulled off. Or —had merely worked loose and fallen off? In that case, it might be anywhere. It might be on the closet floor.

Until she had looked for the label in the evening dress, and found it gone, and then found it gone in the second dress, Barbara's interest had been idle—the passing interest of one woman in the source of another woman's clothes. But now the interest was active, since the implication was obvious. The labels had been removed to hamper identification of the girl who had died under the name of Nora Evans, but might at some time have lived under another.

Barbara groped for, and found, a dangling cord in the closet, and pulled at it, and a small bulk in the ceiling went on. She crouched and began to search the floor. She was searching, handicapped by the darkness of her own shadow, when she heard sounds from the living room. She stood up—

There was the sound of something heavy falling to a padded surface—the sound of feet running on the padded surface. Then there was a muffled exclamation, wordless—a kind of involuntary "uh!" And then, again, there was a sound of someone running on a carpeted floor.

By then, Barbara was herself running—out of the closet, across the room, to the door of the living room.

The room was dark, except for the light which flowed into it in a narrow path from the open bedroom door—a path of light in which her own shadow was large, distorted.

"John!" she called. "*John!*"

There was no answer. She went into the dark room and called again, and now there was something near panic in her voice.

But then she heard the sound of a door closing, and almost at once the lights came on in the room.

John walked from the entrance door of the apartment, down the steps to the sunken living room. As he came toward her, he rubbed his forehead with the heel of his right hand.

"Got away," John said. "Must have gone down the stairs."

"Are you all right?" she said. "Tell me. *Are you all right?*"

"What?" he said, and then, "Oh, sure. I'm all right. He got the photograph. Rammed into me. Knocked me into a chair or something. Grabbed the picture and—"

He walked past her quickly, to the door to the kitchen; the door at the far end of the living room. He was there only a moment. He reached up to the wall and there was the click of a light switch and the lights went out. Almost at once, the switch clicked again, and there was light. He walked back to her.

"Hiding in the kitchen," he said. "There's a three-way switch. Turn the lights on and off from either end of the room. Then—he ran for it. Knocked me out of the way. He was on me before I heard him. I chased him, but he got away."

"You're not hurt?" she said.

"No." He paused. "What would anybody want in the kitchen?"

Barbara shook her head quickly.

"Come here," she said. "It wasn't what he was doing in the kitchen."

83

He followed her into the bedroom. She showed him what she had found. She held up the green dress. "Except for this one," she said. "This one whoever it was didn't cut. Merely jerked at. Unless—"

They had not heard footsteps. They heard only a voice, from the doorway. It was a hard voice, without inflection. "Keeping busy?" the voice said.

They turned. Detective Grady was in the doorway. Shapiro was behind him. Grady answered his own question, in the same voice. "Keeping real busy, aren't they, Nate?" he said. "Taking care of evidence, wouldn't you say, Nate? Who are you, lady?"

"Barbara Phillips," she said. "And who are you, gentlemen?"

"He's Grady," John said, before Grady answered. "Grady and Shapiro."

Barbara Phillips said, "Oh," with a careful avoidance of cordiality.

"So," Grady said, "you're the Phillips girl. She's the Phillips girl, Nate." He looked at her. He looked very carefully, as if at an object. "Gets around, doesn't he?" Grady said. "Get around, don't you, Mr. Hayward?"

Involuntarily, John took a step toward him. "No!" Barbara said and Grady said, "The lady's right, Mr. Hayward." John stopped. "So," Grady said, "you used the key. We thought you might. Didn't we, Nate? But you didn't wear the jacket. Showy thing, the jacket."

"Yeah," Detective Shapiro said, in his soft sad voice. "We thought you might, Mr. Hayward."

"I suppose," John said, "that that's why you put it there? The jacket with the key in the pocket?"

"You get funny ideas," Grady said. "Don't he, Nate?"

Shapiro, this time, merely nodded, sadly.

"What would we put it there for?" Grady said. "You can do better than that, can't you? It was there when we—" He stopped. "We knew it was there," he said.

"When you searched my apartment," John said.

84

A little elaborately, Grady pantomimed astonished innocence. Then he was reproachful. "You know we'd have to have a search warrant," he said. "Anybody serve a warrant on you, Mr. Hayward? How you going to prove we were there? Anybody see us there?"

"All right," John said, "you can see through walls."

"On the other hand," Grady said, "you're here, aren't you? Revisiting the scene, they call it. Anybody say you could come here?"

"According to you," John said, "I was paying the rent. You can't have it both ways, can you?"

As a triumph it was small, but in its small way satisfying.

"Smart cooky, isn't he, Nate?" Grady said. "We're horsing around. You like to horse around, Mr. Hayward?"

John said nothing.

"The labels on the dresses," Grady said. "That was a cute one. Afraid we'll find out who the girl was, Mr. Hayward? Check back on her, from where she bought the stuff? Not a bad idea. Thought he might try that, or something like it, didn't we, Nate?"

This time, Shapiro said, "Yeah."

"Something like that," Grady said. "And that nice picture of him. What did you do with the picture, Mr. Hayward? And the dress labels? You and Miss Phillips here. Down the incinerator chute outside?"

"No," John said. "Somebody got here ahead of us. And— was still here when we came. You—I'd think you'd have run into him."

Grady sighed, deeply.

"Mr. Whoseit," Grady said. "The same old gag. All right, Mr. Hayward. You tell it."

John told it. He told it, evidently, to disbelieving ears.

"Quite a story," Grady said. "You see this—this man of mystery, Miss Phillips? Have green hair, or anything? Easy to pick up, if he had green hair."

"You're really very cute," Barbara said. "You work at it very hard."

85

"Lady," Grady said, "your papa runs a bank. You're an important young lady. Did you see this man you say got the picture? You say got the labels?"

"No," she said. "I was in here. I was looking on the closet floor. I thought maybe he'd dropped one. I heard sounds. Someone running. When I got to the door, he'd got away."

"No green hair," Grady said. "That's too bad. Did you make some noises for the lady, Mr. Hayward? Struggle noises? Running noises?"

"No," John said. "But it's no good, is it? You and Miller've got it all worked out."

"Yeah," Grady said. "That's right. All worked out. Oh—we made a list of the labels. Got a policewoman to describe the dresses and things they were on. Checked them out. Some very nice stores the boys and girls have been visiting. And you know what? Ones we can check back on, Miss Evans bought. Paid cash. So now we know that. And that nice picture of you. We made copies of that. Several copies. So you don't have to worry about having it grabbed that way."

"And," John said, "left everything here hoping someone would—come around to tidy up? That's the way you work it?"

"One of the ways," Grady said. "We've got lots of ways, haven't we, Nate? And—surprise surprise—look who came to tidy up. Knocks us over with a fender, like the lady used to say on the radio. Don't it, Nate?"

But Nathan Shapiro had wandered off. They could, after a moment, hear him. He appeared to be in the kitchen.

"Don't take anything for granted. That's Detective Shapiro," Grady said. "Maybe, he thinks, this man of yours left a card or something. Benefit-of-the-doubt-Shapiro."

"For you," Barbara said, "there isn't any doubt, is there?"

"Nope," Grady said. "If I had my way—" He stopped.

There was no need for him to continue. He was explicit enough, in words, in tone.

"But the trouble is," John said, "you don't even know if her name was Evans."

"O.K.," Grady said. "You're a very smart cooky. Everybody admits you're a very smart cooky. Now you've got a very smart lady helping—very smart, important young lady, whose papa owns a bank." He raised his voice. "Nate," he said, and Shapiro came in. Shapiro shook his head.

"Not a chance in a hundred," Grady said, "but let's see if they've got them on them."

"Turn your pockets out, Mr. Hayward," Shapiro said. "Let's see if you've got 'em."

Hayward took articles from his pockets, turned the pockets inside out. Shapiro ran expert hands over him. He said, "Nope."

"Like I said," Grady said, "probably the incinerator." He looked at Barbara. A lightweight woolen dress molded her slender body. She looked at him steadily. "O.K.," Grady said, "we'll settle for your bag." Her bag was on a chest of drawers. She emptied it on the top of the chest of drawers. "O.K.," Grady said. "We go through the forms. All right. Get going. Don't come back."

Barbara went first out of the bedroom. "Figure," Grady told John Hayward, "that your lease has expired. And—I'll take that key." John gave him the key.

"Oh yes," Grady said, "we showed that jacket to some people. Pedersen, one of them was. Said you wore it when you came here, part of the time."

"I thought you didn't—" John began, and was interrupted; was told to be his age.

"Found it there," Grady said. "Two of us—Nate and me. We can swear to that. If we took it away and showed it to some people and put it back—but who says we did that, Mr. Hayward? We say it was there first night when we picked it up. When you let us in. See how it figures?"

"In other words, you're willing to lie."

"Who says? A man who strangles a girl half his size? A girl, maybe, coming to him to be kissed?"

He looked at John, and looked at him with hatred.

"Get going," Grady said. "While you can."

87

There was, John thought, no use going on with it—not with Grady. He and Barbara walked the length of the living room, with the detectives watching them, Grady implacable, and Shapiro looking very, very sad.

"We only made it worse," John said, when they were in a cab, going up Fifth. "Now Grady is surer than ever."

"But," Barbara said, "someone isn't. Because they don't know who the girl is." Then she said, "It's cold, isn't it. Put your arms around me." He put his arms around her. She was trembling. But it was not really cold.

She quieted in his arms. She was herself again when they reached the Phillips house—a house set shoulder to shoulder with its neighbors but, as such houses go in New York, broad of shoulder. It was taken for granted that he would come in with her. He followed her in.

Stairs ran up from the entrance hall. To the right of the hall, beyond a wide doorway, was the library. Martin Phillips sat in a deep chair, under a light. He took off his glasses and laid them on a book open in his lap. Then, rather slowly, he laid book and glasses on a table and stood up.

"Well," John said, "it was no good, sir. You were right, and I promised but—it was no good."

"Evidently," Martin Phillips said. "Very evidently. She is too much for both of us. And—too much to be protected."

"It wasn't ever," Barbara said, "not ever, one of your better ideas, father."

"Perhaps not," Martin Phillips said. He looked from one to the other, longest at his daughter.

"Facts don't mean anything, do they?" he said. He looked at John. "Is she right, Hayward?"

"There's no reason you should believe it," John said. "But she's right."

"If she's wrong," Phillips said, "it will be a very bad thing. For everybody. And, most of all for you." He turned back to Barbara. "You are quite sure?" he said.

"Yes," Barbara said. "There isn't any possible doubt."

For some seconds, then, father and daughter looked at each other. Finally, Phillips slowly nodded his massive head.

"It's nothing we can go beyond, apparently," he said. "And —nothing I would want to change if I could." He turned again to John. "You're very lucky," he said. "I hope not luckier than you deserve."

He said, "Good night," then, and went out of the room. They could hear him climbing the stairs, steadily, not rapidly. . . .

On his way home in a cab, John thought of a tree—a tree seen distantly, in full leaf, hazy in a background. If I could remember the tree, he thought. I have to remember the tree. Methodically, he tried to picture the places where, the summer before, he had gone to play tennis. Or—had dressed as if for tennis. Because a tennis shirt did not necessarily mean—

The telephone was ringing when he went into his apartment.

"The green dress," Barbara said. "You remember? The one the label wasn't cut out of?"

For a moment he did not. Then he said, "Yes."

"I remember it," she said. "I almost bought it. And—it was late in August. Last August. Fall things were just beginning to come in. Do you see?"

"Before the apartment was rented," he said. "Yes, I see. It's —it's a little thing, though."

"Big or little," she said. "It's a thing. We need things. Listen—"

He listened.

VII

MME. JACQUES' WAS "a little place on Madison Avenue." All New York women know little places on Madison Avenue; many of them know several. Mme. Jacques' had a single dress in its single window. It had a narrow door and the door was curtained. It was, John Hayward thought, quite irrelevantly, the sort of door at which one felt one should knock. It seemed discourteous, intrusive, merely to open the door and walk in. John opened the door and walked in.

Barbara was not yet there. A middle-aged woman with beautifully ordered, and slightly blueish, gray hair advanced delicately on the carpeted floor. She was a substantial woman, but corsets allowed her figure no nonsense. She said, "Yes?" on a rising note.

"I'm meeting Miss—" John began, and Barbara Phillips came in.

"Miss *Phillips!*" the middle-aged woman said, to one long-awaited, highly prized.

The woman was not Mme. Jacques. Mme. Jacques was Max Jackman, who was roly-poly, uncorseted, and backstage. The woman was Mary Callahan.

"Such a long time we haven't seen you," Mary Callahan said, with reproach not to be taken seriously. "You're looking so lovely, my dear."

But she was not looking so much at Barbara as at Barbara's spring coat; at the bright print under it.

"Such a gay little frock, too," Mary Callahan said, proving herself generous, since the dress was not a Mme. Jacques'. She felt she could afford to be generous—when pretty young women of notable financial standing brought young men, probably of the same, with them—"Well," Mary Callahan thought. "Boy. Oh *boy!*" "We have some *lovely* things," Mary Callahan said. "Only this morning I was saying, 'That's the very thing for Miss Phillips. Something not everybody could wear, but on her—' "

She stopped with the air of one who, in the throes of uncontrollable enthusiasm, feels she is talking too much.

"But I'm rattling on," Mary Callahan said. "I know you must have something special in mind." She looked quickly at John. "She has such *wonderful* taste," she said. "But I'm sure I'm not telling you anything you don't know."

"Um-m," John Hayward said.

"Mary," Barbara said, "I want you to help me. I'll buy your very nicest frock tomorrow. Or day after tomorrow."

Mary Callahan raised her eyebrows a little, with the air of one who listens. Mary Callahan's face changed. It seemed to John Hayward to become more really a face.

"Late last summer," Barbara said. "August, I think it was. You had a dress—a little woolen dress. It came in green and blue and, I think, in black."

Mary Callahan listened. She waited. It would, John thought, be hopeless. Nobody would remember a single dress out, he supposed, of hundreds.

"I almost bought it," Barbara said. "But then, instead, I decided on a suit dress—gray and blue. With lovely detail on the jacket. Little tucks?"

"It was charming on you," Mary Callahan said. "You didn't make a mistake."

"Lovely," Barbara said. "But then, all your things are."

Mary Callahan's face looked more than ever like a face.

"The one I didn't get," Barbara said. "The little woolen thing. Here it went—"

Barbara had taken off her spring coat. Now, her quick, slender hands moved. They moved at her neck and breast, describing a pattern in the air in front of her. "And there—" now her hands moved closer to her hips. "Tucked, just a little," Barbara said. "But the thing I liked best—" She turned, and her quick hands seemed to smooth the air in the area of her small, neat buttocks. "None of that pull-in," Barbara said.

"It would be difficult to find a dress that—would on you,"

Mary Callahan said. Then, "Wait. I think I remember. The sleeves—"

And now she, less quickly, with less grace, but quite as decisively, made air patterns. She had pretty, plump hands, with short red nails. John supposed that, in this strange fashion, woman to woman, they communicated. It appeared they did.

"That's it," Barbara said. "I knew you'd remember."

"A little dress," Mary Callahan said. "Not important at all. Just a little thing you'd live in."

"Yes," Barbara said, and nodded her head. "Oh—not over fifty dollars."

"Fifty-four ninety-five," Mary Callahan said. "But—" She paused, seemed puzzled. "It's nothing you want for now," she said. "And by the time you do—"

"No," Barbara said. "I want to know who you sold them to."

Mary Callahan looked more puzzled than before; she looked doubtful.

"Please," Barbara said. "It's—it could be important, Mary. Did other shops have the dress?"

"Exclusive with us," Mary Callahan said. "Not an important dress, but exclusive." She paused. "In the area," she added. "They went very fast, as I remember it. Of course, we never stock many of any number. You know that."

"Of course," Barbara said. "It's one reason so many of us— I mean, it does give one confidence."

"It's something you can count on," Mary Callahan said. "I don't suppose—oh, more than four or five. In a dress of that type—a little dress. In something more important, it would be only the one, you know. Unless, that is, we made it a special order."

Barbara nodded. She waited.

"I suppose I could find out," Mary Callahan said. "Ordinarily—you say it's important?"

"Very important," Barbara said. "Oh, very important. And —it doesn't matter about the eighteens. Or even the sixteens. The one I'm interested in was a ten. In the green." She

93

paused, momentarily. "I'd appreciate it so much," she said.

"If it was a charge," Mary Callahan said. "Or someone who's a regular. If someone merely walked in off the street—" She raised plump shoulders. "But that seldom happens," she said. "With us, you know."

It appeared that Barbara did know. John merely stood. It went on around him.

"Wait," Mary Callahan said, and went back through the shop—which had only two dresses on display, on figures; which was a very reticent shop. She pushed aside a curtain, and vanished.

"Does she," John said, "really know the dress you mean?"

He was looked at in surprise; a neat, small head was shaken in surprise.

"Of course," Barbara said. "I described it very clearly." But for an instant, and for the first time since long before, there was laughter in her widely spaced brown eyes. She sobered instantly.

"You're all right?" she said. "There hasn't been anything else."

"Nothing else," he said.

"About the photograph?"

He could only shake his head.

"It will come back," she said.

They waited, standing side by side, not touching—and as if their arms were about one another.

Mary Callahan came back after about ten minutes; she smiled and nodded as she came through the shop, vouching for success. She said it had not taken her long, had it? She had a slip of paper, with names written on it.

"Max was a little stuffy, just at first," Mary Callahan said. "But I told him it was Miss *Phillips*, so of course—" She handed Barbara the slip of paper.

"One of each size," she said. "Ten through sixteen. It wasn't made in eighteen, except on a special order. We did reorder on the fourteen—a green, as it happens. But, it's all there."

Barbara looked at the names on the slip of paper.

94

"The ten green," she said. "Martha Blake. I know Martha." This was to John. "The twelve—it might just have been a twelve, although I don't think so. Mrs—" She hesitated over the name for a moment. "Mrs. Leroy Slipperton?"

"One of our best customers," Mary Callahan said. "Such a lovely little thing. Such a delightful figure. Like yours, my dear. Except just here." She touched her own body in the area of the waist. "As it happens, they all went to very good customers. We didn't show it to everyone."

Barbara handed the slip back. She shook her head.

"It isn't what you wanted," Mary Callahan said. "Oh dear. I'm so sorry."

"I want," Barbara Phillips said, "a girl with red hair. A— a girl who's dead now, Mary."

"Not—" Mary said. "Then you're—" She did not finish this, either. She looked at John Hayward. There was, he thought, nothing but curiosity in her blue eyes.

"Yes," he said.

"I'm so sorry," Mary Callahan said. "So dreadfully sorry. But—I know all these." She fluttered the slip in plump fingers. "None of them is—is the girl you're talking about."

"No," Barbara said. "Well, I appreciate what you've done, Mary. We—it was just a chance. You're quite sure the dress was exclusive?"

"Yes," Mary Callahan said. "Only with us. Of course, our Danbury shop—I think several did go up there."

* * *

We must look very carefree, Barbara Phillips thought; we must look very young and gay, in a young, gay car in a bright spring world. It isn't—how did Grandfather Rickford use to phrase it? It isn't seemly. (So many things had not been, for Grandfather Rickford.) She felt, for almost the first time in her life, that something might be said for the point of view. A black sedan, with the windows closed—that would be seemly. Not this bright, sleek little car, skimming the parkways, with the top down. A day of gray rain; that would be seemly. Not this sunny day of spring, with each forsythia bush along the Hutchinson River Parkway itself a little sun; not this day, with the world dressed up for spring.

Beside her, John drove the Corvette. His face was set; he looked only at the road. Of course, he always drove with concentration. But usually he smiled as he drove—smiled at the road, and at the little car which skimmed it. Well, there was nothing to smile about. And yet, she thought again, we must, to people who look at us, look so carefree. Like a bright young couple in an advertisement. For a moment, and as a kind of escape from the anxiety which rode with them, she thought of the young people, the boys and girls, and the elder people of distinction, who were photographed for such advertisements—advertisements for whiskies, and clothes, and automobiles, all of distinction. The boys and girls in the photographs were notably carefree, the elder, at the least, notably contented. And they were, really, people who earned their livings by being photographed; people who must, often, wonder if they would stay young enough and gay enough, or distinguished enough, to go on earning.

"Russ Norton," John said, lifting his voice a little, because the rushing air tossed words away. "What sort is he?"

"Not mine," she said. "As it turned out. A little—" She paused for a word. "Well," she said, "devious. In a straightforward, Ivy League way. But it wasn't that, so much. He was so very—sure of himself."

"And," he said, "of you?"

"It was," she said, "rather like being something he'd invented. Or—it would have been. It didn't go far, John. There was no reason to drag things out."

He did not look away from the road. Even without looking at each other, she thought, we're beginning to hear things not actually said. By the time we've been married years—ten years, fifty years—we'll communicate entirely by osmosis. Which will be a little odd, but wonderful.

"I barely know him," John said. "He took it hard?"

"Grimly," she said. "The very stiff upper lip."

"Underneath?"

"Annoyed," she said. "But, only partly because of me, I'm afraid. The rest because father has such a pleasant amount of money. But—he'd know that getting rid of you wouldn't make any difference. Not that kind of difference. Anyway, it's—"

She did not finish. He waited for her to finish. But then he said, "Preposterous. I know. But the whole thing is."

For some time, then, he merely drove the little car through the brightness of spring. They stopped and paid toll, and the man in the toll booth smiled at them. Because, she thought, we look so young and gay. They drove on.

"There has to be some reason," John said. "It won't ever seem good enough. Norton—of course it's preposterous. Hank Roberts? Because one of us will, maybe, be a vice president some day, but not both, and he thinks 'Better me than him.' That's preposterous. Al Curtis? I can't think of any reason, preposterous or not. Dick Still? It's the same thing."

He spoke with pauses; the wind tossed his words away. At times, the needs of driving interrupted him.

"They're the ones who might have known I couldn't account for Saturday afternoon," he said, and went around a slow-moving car. They were on the Merritt Parkway by then, shooting up and down hill on the wide, smooth pavement of that perilous highway.

He was told he had forgotten Mr. Woodson and at that, for the first time, John laughed. It was brief laughter. "Because I took him out of a business double?" he said. "Or didn't respond to a four no-trump?"

After some time, he added that none of it made sense. And then, that, sense or not, it had happened—was happening.

"The girl," he said, "and a green dress—that maybe she bought last summer. Maybe in Danbury."

"A place to start," she said. "If it's wrong, we'll find another."

They drove for some time in silence, then. We haven't

97

much, she thought; he's right we haven't much. A green dress. The outline of a tree in the background of a photograph. And they have so much—a name on a check and laundry marks on shirts and a fat man who says, "Yes, that's Mr. Hayward."

(The car which followed closest was just such a black sedan as Barbara had thought would be more seemly than the small, bright Corvette. The car which followed the sedan was a several-year-old Jaguar, with the top up. But the Corvette followed many cars ahead; behind it, on the busy road, cars followed endlessly on. The stream of cars was without end or beginning. They reached the intersection with Route 7, and left the Parkway and went north. The black sedan turned behind them. So, but a considerable distance back, did the Jaguar.)

A little way beyond Ridgefield, having by-passed the village itself, John slowed the car, and looked at the watch on his wrist. It was a little after one; they had not driven fast; it had taken time, after they had left Mme. Jacques', to pick up John's car, to wheedle their way through city traffic.

"Lunch?" John said, and when she nodded, he turned the car at a sign which read, "Fox Hill, an Inn." They climbed a winding road to a spreading building—a mansion of the past. They had a cocktail on a sweep of lawn, with what seemed half of Connecticut laid out before them. The trees were lacy with spring—spring seemed caught, a tinted haze on winter branches.

(The black sedan did not turn after them, but pulled in at a lunchroom on Route 7, almost opposite the inlet road to Fox Hill. The Jaguar checked slightly, and then went on.)

It was after two when John found a parking space on Danbury's main street. They walked half a block to "Mme. Jacques'." The Danbury shop was less reticent than its parent; there were several dresses in the window, and the door was uncurtained.

This time, Barbara had the stock number of the green dress, and its maker's name. But, this time, the dress was not remembered; this time, Barbara Phillips was merely a girl in a spring dress (not from Mme. Jacques') in the company of a tall man who looked perfectly all right, but like everybody. So there was delay; there was a telephone call, for authorization, to Madison Avenue. (After that, there was much less reluctance, and much busying among files.)

Only three of the dresses had been sold in Danbury. Two of them had been bought by known customers. But the third —a size ten, in green—had been sold for cash. The salesgirl shook her head. "I wasn't even here then," she said, but then she said, "Wait," and went into the rear of the shop. She came back with an older woman.

There had been discussion of an alteration, which the old lady had suggested, out of which she had been talked, by the fitter and the girl.

"Wait," John said. He took from an envelope in his pocket the sketch of the dead girl, cut from the *World Telegram and Sun*. He showed it to the older woman. "Was this the girl?"

The woman looked at it; she held it so that the light fell on it. Finally, she shook her head, slowly. "It's not much to go by," she said. "Anyway, it was a long time ago." She held the picture out, still shaking her head. "Could be," she said. "But, if she walked in here this moment, I couldn't swear to anything. As for this—" She shrugged. John took the reproduced sketch. He put it back in the envelope.

"Did she have red hair?" Barbara asked.

The woman thought a moment. She said she thought perhaps she had had. She could not be sure. It was evident that she remembered the "old lady" more clearly—the old lady in her eighties, leaning on a cane; the old lady dressed in black, with sharp black eyes. She was thin and, although stooped, still tall—much taller than the girl.

Neither the old lady nor the girl had, so far as could be remembered, before visited Mme. Jacques'. If names had been given—but there was no particular reason they should have been; the dress was carried away—they had long since been forgotten.

99

"But the girl might have had red hair," Barbara said, on the sidewalk outside. "They shopped in Danbury."

Many people shop in Danbury; it is a small, but busy city. It was not a needle in a haystack; it was a tiny end of string, projecting from a tangle, something to be pulled at. But it seemed to have slipped from their fingers.

They separated for the search, for the asking of questions of busy clerks; they met blank faces and shaking heads, and a reticence based on suspicion. Other clothing shops had at first seemed most likely, but half a dozen produced nothing. It was Barbara who suggested that, after such shops, drugstores should come next. Women in their eighties may be presumed to be often in need of medication.

There were many drugstores, and they went to the wrong ones first, and it was almost six when John, asking familiar questions of an elderly clerk in a small, and sedate, apothecary's (so termed) on a side street, was answered slowly, doubtfully, with the possibility that "it might be the old lady is Mrs. Piermont. Except, she lives pretty near over to Brewster. Shops there, mostly, I guess."

But at long intervals, if something brought her to Danbury, old Mrs. Piermont came to the apothecary's shop; came for a proprietary no longer advertised, nor much stocked. Could be this was old Mrs. Piermont. A girl—once he had seen a girl. Or thought perhaps he had. At other times, Mrs. Piermont had been alone.

Brewster, which is not far from Danbury, and in New York, is a village, with a main street and a railway station. They were late at Brewster. The post office, of which John had thought first, was closed. They tried one of the two drugstores. They were trying to find a Mrs. Piermont, John told a quick, dry, small man at the prescription counter. "Old Mrs. Piermont?" the man said. Then he added, "Not that there's a young Mrs. Piermont. Lives up on Ridge Hill. Lived there a hundred years, more or less."

"Less, surely," Barbara said, and was laughed with, was told "not a lot less." Somewhat hastily, the small, quick man, added that Mrs. Piermont was a great old girl and then, by way of correction, that she was a mighty fine old lady. Then, he waited, with curiosity.

"A friend of my grandfather's," Barbara said. "Isn't there a girl lives with her? A red-haired girl?"

"The Titus girl," the druggist said. "That'd be the one. Right pretty, considering."

They waited. He did not amplify.

"Ridge Hill?" John said. "How do we get there?"

They were told. They went back for a mile or two on Route 6, turned right on Ridge Road, turned off Ridge Road, again, to the right, at a white house, climbed a hill and turned right once more. A dirt road, that would be, but ought to be all right now. Two weeks ago—but it wasn't two weeks ago. Dry enough now.

Reached, it was dry enough—narrow and tortuous, but the little car was nimble. A driveway, finally, led to the left, opposite a small mailbox marked, simply, "Piermont." Partially, through close-growing trees, they could see, several hundred feet back from the road, a large, gray-painted house. Much more clearly, and closer, they could see a heavy chain across the driveway. John pulled the car to the side of the road. He got out and examined the chain. One end was fixed to a ring in a metal post; the other padlocked to a similar post. But, on the drive beyond, there were the tracks of a car. Barbara joined him.

"We've come this far," John said, and they ducked under the chain. The driveway wound, and climbed. They went a hundred feet, and a man's voice said, "Looking for somebody?" There was no welcome in the voice.

He was a rangy, weathered man. He held a long pole, with pruning sheers fastened at the end.

"Mrs. Piermont," John said.

"Can see she ain't here," the man said. "What'd you think the chain was for?"

"It's important we see her," John said.

101

"Ain't here," the man said. "So how you gonna see her, mister?"

"If you could tell us—" Barbara began.

"Florida," the man said. "Be back next month."

"And," Barbara said, "Miss Titus?"

He looked at her.

"What about the Titus girl?" he asked.

"Is she here?"

He looked at Barbara slowly before he answered. Then he said, "Nope."

"With Mrs. Piermont?"

Again he was slow in answering. Then he said, "You got a lot of questions, haven't you? Told you nobody's here. What more do you want?"

"To know where Miss Titus is," John said. "In Florida?"

"Where would she be?" the man said. "Sure she's in Florida." He paused again. "You want to see them so bad," he said, "whyn't you go to Florida?"

He turned, and walked off a few paces, and looked up at a tree. He raised his long pole and snipped at a branch. The branch fell. Then he turned and looked at them. "Get out," he said. "You understand English, don't you?"

They went. He watched them down the drive, under the chain barrier.

⁂

They were watched, also, and from beyond a stone fence, by a man who had parked a black sedan around a bend beyond the Piermont driveway. When he saw them start toward the road, he walked for a short distance behind the fence, and then went over it and back to the sedan. He hoped, absently, that the stuff growing on the wall would not turn out to be what they called poison ivy. He had heard of poison ivy, but he didn't know what it looked like.

He had turned the car, so that it was headed back the way they had come—the way the Corvette had come, and he after

102

it. Presumably, they would turn and go back that way. He waited in the car, and heard the Corvette's motor start.

It had been quite an expedition—into the country, which was a nuisance; into Danbury, where it was almost as difficult to park as in New York—more difficult, for him. He had loitered on foot from dress shop to dress shop, and drugstore to drugstore until finally, apparently, they had found what they wanted. He had been lucky to get back to the sedan in time to follow them to Brewster, and now to this house, occupied—or any rate claimed—by someone named Piermont.

There would be a good deal of backtracking to be done; a good deal of checking out. He had a guess as to what they were up to, and, if he was right, somebody had slipped up in Eleventh Street—which Miller wouldn't like. On the other hand, it might be that work was being done without having to be paid for, a thing to which nobody would object.

Abruptly, Detective Nathan Shapiro slid his long body as low as he could in the front seat of the sedan, and pulled his hat as low as he conveniently could over his face, so that he looked like a man dozing in his car. At any rate, he hoped he did; it would be a nuisance if he looked dead, and the occupants of the Corvette—which had not turned and gone back, but had continued in the way it was headed—got out to investigate.

They did not. They were talking as they went by, and only glanced at the sedan, pulled off the narrow road.

Shapiro had to drive back to the Piermont drive, and turn in it, nosing up to the chain, before he could follow. With the time so lost, it would be easy enough for the Corvette to ditch him—if it wanted to. The country was a hell of a place, and full of noisy birds.

VIII

IT HAD BEEN Barbara who suggested that, instead of turning back, they might as well go on. "Since we don't know where we're going anyway," John said.

"Roads always lead somewhere," she said. "Little roads lead to larger roads."

"Or," John said, "to farmers' barnyards."

But he started the Corvette and they went on up the winding road. They passed a black sedan, drawn to the side of the road, with a man sleeping in it. He didn't look too comfortable, Barbara said, and they said no more, and thought no more, of that.

"The girl was named Titus," Barbara said. "We know that much."

But they did not; not certainly. It was still, he said, intangible. All tangibility was, still, on the other side. They would fix that, she told him. Oh, surely, they would fix that.

She was right, at any rate, about the road. It dead-ended at a wider road. "We could flip a coin," John said, and, without bothering to, turned to the left. And, almost at once, they were in a village—the smallest and neatest of villages—a dozen white houses spaced along the road; a single, but general, store; a filling station with only two pumps and without blatancy. And—a church with a white spire. They drove slowly, the low sun in their eyes, through this tiny, pleasant place. And then Barbara said, "Wait, John," and pointed.

In front of the church was a reticent sign, black lettered on white—lettered, "St. Matthew's (Episcopal.)" But it was not at that Barbara pointed. In front of the white house next the church, there was another sign, even smaller, more sedate. The sign read, "The Rectory."

"Well?" John said, but further slowed the little car.

"Somebody to ask," she said. "Somebody who would know —almost surely would know."

105

John pulled the car to the side of the road, and, after a moment, cut the motor.

"You mean," he said, "we just barge in? Say, 'Who's this Miss Titus? Is she a girl with red hair? Not in Florida, but dead and in the morgue?'"

"There is," she told him, "only one way to find things out. Only one way I've ever heard of."

She was out of the car. To John, following her, she seemed to twinkle in the slanting light of evening.

The road, here, was lined with trees—maple trees, and very old. Suddenly, as he followed the girl under one of the trees, up to the door of the white rectory, John thought: The tree by the tennis court is a maple tree. He looked up at the tree under which he was walking. A tree like this—I can almost see it. But then, as quickly as this certainty had come, it passed, and he could not see the tree by the tennis court, or remember where it grew. After this, John Hayward thought, I'll look at things. By God, but I'll look at things.

* * *

The narrow, winding road dead-ended at a wider, straighter road. Detective Nathan Shapiro stopped the small black sedan and looked hopefully for road signs. He was, he discovered, at the end of Elm Lane. He could go right or left on Briggs Hill Road. But where he would come out, in which-ever way he turned, was not revealed. He could flip a coin. He turned right. If his hunch—it was only that—proved out, this way would take him back to Brewster. Whether it would take him in further pursuit of the Corvette was anybody's guess.

Whether it had remained anybody's guess, but the point became academic. Whichever way they had gone, they had shaken him, by intention or by chance. He thought the latter; he was quite certain they had not recognized him when he slumped low in the seat of the sedan, like a man asleep. He did not think they had had any idea they were being followed.

He drove a mile or so. He encountered only one other car—a Jaguar, top up, occupant almost obscured, bound in the opposite direction at, for a Jaguar, a discreet speed. It was, Detective Shapiro thought vaguely, getting so you saw a lot of those about. And damned uncomfortable they looked.

The road turned, and the countryside opened. He was on a hill, with Brewster below him and the road easing down toward the village. Here and there, although needlessly, there were already lights in the village.

The Corvette was nowhere in sight on the straight downslope. Well, he had not supposed it would be. He rolled down the gentle hill, through the gentle countryside, toward Brewster, and a telephone.

* * *

The door was opened before they knocked. A man in black, with a clerical collar, opened the door wide and stood in the doorway. He was not a tall man, and he was plump. He appeared to be in his sixties. His plump face was rosy; he took off glasses and looked out through gentle (and obviously myopic) eyes.

"I am Father Higbee," he said. "I seem to be wearing the wrong glasses. Do come in."

He stood back, holding the door open. They went in. He took them into what appeared to be a study. Small windows were open, and the spring air stirred softly in the room. Father Higbee went behind a desk, and peered down at it. "Ah," he said, and picked up another pair of glasses. He removed the glasses he wore and put on the others. He looked at Barbara and John through the new glasses.

"At this time of the day," Father Higbee said, and spoke gently, "I customarily have a cocktail." He looked at his desk. There was a partially empty glass on it. "Indeed," he said, "I was having a cocktail. A martini. Of course, if you"—this was to Barbara—"would prefer a cup of tea?"

"Father Higbee," John said, "you never saw us before. You don't know why we have come."

"In good time," Father Higbee said. "All in good time."

"A martini," Barbara said, "would be very pleasant, Father. My name is Barbara Phillips. This is John Hayward."

"Ah," Father Higbee said, but it did not seem probable he had heard. He had turned to a cabinet behind him; had taken from it a cocktail mixer, and bottles, and from a container, ice cubes. He measured carefully, but evidently by color. He poured into fresh glasses and then, abstractedly, filled his own glass.

"At the end of the day," Father Higbee said, "the creature comforts." He raised his glass, and they raised theirs. The drinks had the appearance, but by no means the flavor, of water. "Possibly," Father Higbee said, "a touch too much vermouth?"

He was reassured; he was quickly reassured.

"I felt," Father Higbee said, "that I had not met you before. Either of you. You are new to Saint Matthew's Parish? It is pleasant to see new young faces."

"Father," John said, "we are looking for information."

"Ah," Father Higbee said. "I had thought perhaps you planned to get married."

"Oh," Barbara said, "we do. But—not today."

"You will like being married," Father Higbee said, and smiled at her, but then the smile faded on the rosy, friendly face. "My own dear wife and I were happy for many years." He put down his half-empty glass and looked at it, as if, somehow, it puzzled him. "However," he said. "If I can help you in any way?"

"We—" Barbara began, but John said, "No. Wait, Barbara," and then, "Father Higbee, a girl was killed last Saturday. In New York. The police think I killed her. I didn't kill her. We are trying to find out who she was."

Father Higbee looked at John, steadily, and for some time.

"Tell me how I can help you, John," he said, finally.

John told him. At the end, he showed him the newspaper picture. As the woman at the dress shop had done, the round-faced clergyman looked at the picture, holding it to the light. He changed his glasses and looked at it again. And, then he, too, shook his head. He said it was very hard to be sure.

"Actually," he said, "it could be almost anyone, couldn't it? Any pretty young woman. It might be Julie Titus—that is her name. Julie. But from this, I doubt whether anyone could be sure." He gave the picture back. "And," he said, "I've only seen Julie once or twice since—since she became a young woman."

They looked at him. He nodded slowly.

"She is very rarely seen by anyone," the priest said. "For —for reasons which seemed adequate to Angela." He paused. "Angela Piermont," he said. "She has done a great deal for Julie. She is a good woman, John. Whatever she did was for the best. But—it left the girl very unprepared. I have ventured to tell Angela that but Angela—" He paused again. "She knows her own mind, as we say," Father Higbee said.

He sipped from his glass. He said that he could tell them little more than anyone, living for miles around, could tell them of Mrs. Angela Piermont, long a widow, and Julie Titus —"the pretty Titus girl." It was simpler, probably, to begin with the Tituses.

"I can only tell you of the background," he said. "Of events —I know little of events. Angela goes to Florida every year— goes much earlier than most, and stays longer. Angela is very old, and blood thins as we grow old. Or, so we say. The girl goes with her—to Bradenton, I think it is. Somewhere on the Florida west coast, at any rate. I would have supposed they were there now. So, on that I cannot help you. But for the background—"

The Titus family had been long in the area. For two centuries there had been Tituses in that part of Putnam County, in upper Westchester, in adjacent areas of Connecticut.

There had been a Titus who was a governor; there were Tituses who had been judges. "My own great-grandfather was
a Titus," Father Higbee said. "Angela Piermont is a Titus."

"Then the girl—" Barbara said.

"Is a relative?" Father Higbee said. "Yes—of Angela's. In
some degree, perhaps, of mine. But remotely." He paused.
"In a sense," he said, "only the name—the name itself—con-
nects. One could never trace it down. And—Julie is a Briggs
Hill Titus." He paused. He said that, of course, the term
meant nothing to them. Briggs Hill was—"a kind of backwa-
ter." There were many such communities in the country, even
quite close to New York. "Even in Westchester," Father
Higbee said.

By no means all the Tituses had been judges and prosper-
ous merchants and physicians, although some had. Others
had been day laborers, farm hands—and less. Much less. The
Briggs Hill Tituses—

"I do not like categories," Father Higbee said. "We cannot,
as children of one Father, set some aside. But—the Briggs
Hill Tituses have, I'm afraid, interbred for several generations. The results have been—adverse. Julie's father is men-
tally subnormal. Probably, he should be in an institution.
Instead, he is often in jail. He has had ten children. The girls
—there are four girls—are very pretty. The oldest of them is
a prostitute. Two of the others are subnormal. Julie's eldest
brother was—he was convicted of killing a child of six."

Father Higbee paused. He shook his head slowly from side
to side, and the rosiness seemed to have faded in his round
and pleasant face.

"So much is ugly," he said. "So much we have made ugly in
God's world." He sipped from his glass.

"I realize you must find out about the girl," he said. "I
realize its importance to you. Yet—I cling to the hope that
the girl is not Julie Titus. She was a sweet, bright child.
Angela rescued her from Briggs Hill, from—from degrada-
tion. When she was a pretty little girl of ten and one of her
brothers—" He stopped. "We have had enough of those ugly

110

things," he said. "I hope she is not the girl who was killed. But—"

He did not finish. He looked at his cocktail glass, which now was empty. He looked at the mixer, which was empty too.

"I fail as a host," he said. He looked at John and Barbara. His glasses, John noticed, were far thicker than most. The visible world of Father Higbee, John thought, was probably of brief extent, even when he remembered to wear the proper glasses.

"No," Barbara said. "They are very good—but, no."

Father Higbee looked at John. John shook his head. Father Higbee looked again at his own empty glass.

"No doubt you are both right," he said, a little wistfully. "Was—this girl pretty?"

"Yes," John said. "She was a very pretty girl. Although I only saw her dead."

"You are wise," Father Higbee said. "Beauty is in the spirit. Julie was a very pretty child. Dangerously pretty, even at ten." He smiled faintly. "My eyes were stronger then," he said. "It was I who told Angela of the girl. Of—her dangerous prettiness. Angela went to see. I do not know actually what —arrangements—she may have made. She took the girl home with her. Brought the girl up. Educated her."

He paused again. They waited.

"After her husband died," he said, "Angela, for a time, operated a girls' school. A very good school, I believe. She had theories about education. She taught Julie herself. She said, 'She is my responsibility. There is much she must be guarded against.' Angela had given up the school by then. She taught the girl at home. And—kept her at home."

They could, he said, see the reason—see, at any rate, Angela Piermont's reasoning. In rural areas, children are collected in buses and taken to district schools. The buses which would have taken Julie, when she was ten and twelve and fourteen, would also have taken her brothers and sisters from Briggs

111

Hill. But it was precisely from that life that Julie was to be guarded.

"I do not know," he said, "how wise that was. We must live in the world we find. Try to better it, to be sure, but live in it." He paused. "I have not always labored in this quiet vineyard," he added, but almost as if to himself, "A child, particularly, may be too closely guarded."

"You think Julie was?" Barbara asked.

Father Higbee peered at her through the thick glasses.

"It may be," he said—"yes, I think she was. She—" He paused again. Again he looked at his empty glass. He took it from the desk and put it on a shelf behind him. "Since she was ten," he said, "she has lived with an aged woman. A woman who had come to—rather distant terms with life. Who sought nothing more from life."

"The poor child," Barbara said. "She must have been very lonely."

"Yes," the priest said. "And—unprepared, wouldn't you think? She is, probably, about your age—in years. And—knows so little of what you, I imagine, know quite well."

He looked at Barbara.

"As another very pretty girl," he said.

"Yes," Barbara said. "Mrs. Piermont should have been—frightened. Even when they were in Florida?"

"I don't know how they lived there," Father Higbee said. "But—yes, my dear. I should think even in Florida. In a quiet hotel. They would stay in a quiet hotel. And Bradenton is, I believe, a quiet town." He paused again. "Although," he said, "I seem to remember that the Braves train there."

They were both slightly surprised.

"Even a clergyman," he said mildly, "can be interested in baseball. I have an excellent television set." He looked at John. "To which, as you are thinking," he said, "I must sit very close. However—"

He hesitated, as if considering.

"Last summer," he said, "late last summer, Julie met a man. I do not know how, or whether Angela knew about it. I—" He paused again. "It was a little odd," he said. Then he stood up behind his desk.

"If you have not had dinner," he said, "I should like very much to take you to the Walpole Inn." They looked at him, puzzled. "They have good food," he said. "It is a quiet place."

"But," John said, "you were about to tell us about some man."

"I have not forgotten," Father Higbee said. "I am not particularly forgetful." But then he smiled. "Only," he said, "how can one say that? Because, of course, one could so easily forget forgetting. I saw Julie and this young man at the inn. Last October. The leaves were just at their best. But—I should like to show you."

A Corvette is built for two, but three are possible. Father Higbee sat between them, and wore a soft black hat firmly on his head. (Now, Barbara thought, we must look as if we were kidnaping a priest.) It was not far to the inn, which was low and pleasantly dim and, when they arrived, empty. A waiter lighted candles on the tables.

"I think," Father Higbee said, "that we might permit ourselves another drink."

They permitted themselves. They did not try to hurry the pleasant, round-faced clergyman. They sipped very slowly, interrupting themselves to order dinner. Then, Father Higbee said that he was selfish.

"I dislike eating alone," he said. "So often, now, I eat alone. I was alone the evening I saw this man of Julie's. But I need not have brought you here. No doubt you had other plans."

"No," John said. "It's pleasant here."

"Yes," Father Higbee said. "Over week ends it is quite crowded. But during the week— It is not unusual to find it empty. I thought it was that evening. But then I saw a couple. Over there." He pointed. He pointed toward a corner table— a table especially secluded, on which, now, a single candle burned steadily, but very softly. "I—" He paused. "I am afraid they were only shadows to me," he said. "I do not see at any distance. But I nodded to them, as pleasantly as I could." He paused again. "Because, of course," he said, "they might very well have been parishioners. I find it well to be on the safe side. People so often are."

He sipped again.

"The man talked to the girl," he said. "Then she stood up—I think she shook her head first—but then stood up. It was as if he had persuaded her. She came over to my table and the man came with her. He was a man of about your height, John. He was wearing a sports jacket—a rather showy jacket. The girl said she was Julie Titus. She asked if I remembered her. She seemed—a little breathless. As if she had made up her mind to do something, and was doing it quickly. You know what I mean, my dear?"

This was to Barbara. "Yes," Barbara said.

"Yes," Father Higbee said. "She said good evening. Then, all in a breath, she said she wanted me to meet a friend of hers. She said, 'Father, I want you to meet John Hayward.'"

IX

AT FIRST THERE was nothing to say, and they said nothing. They had taken Father Higbee back to his pleasant little house and he had said he was sorry it had come to this. "Yes," John had said, and added, forced himself to add, that Father Higbee had done all he could do. Now John drove the little car toward the west, toward the city, with the lights on against the pale darkness of twilight. And there was nothing to say—nothing for either of them to say. John Hayward looked only at the road. He drove automatically.

I am a puppet, he thought—string-dangled, without the power of decision; with only, at moments, the illusion I decide. I am beaten, he thought and, with that, there came again, the frightening darkness of self-doubt. The puppet master—is he really another man, quite another man, who happens enough to resemble me, who has prepared, long in advance, this dance he leads me? Or—*is he something in myself?* A self, I am, but have forgotten?

Barbara sat beside him, looked at the same road under the lights of the car, was silent as he was silent. Yet, John thought, I am alone. It was this way before, he thought. A long time ago it was this way—

(I wake in a center of loneliness. There are men around me, but they cannot see me, cannot reach me. They say my name. And they say, "*Lieutenant!* Do you hear me, lieutenant?" but they are too distant to be answered; even the air between me and those others has become a barrier. I say, "Yes, I hear you, doctor," but they cannot hear me speak. I—)

"John," Barbara said. "Do you hear me, John? Listen to me, John."

("Hayward," the doctor says. "Listen to me, Hayward. Do you hear me, lieutenant?"

"I hear you," John Hayward said. "Don't you hear me answer, doctor?"

But he did not hear the doctor, who was too far away, who was behind air turned impervious to sound, and the doctor did not hear him. "—be all right," the doctor said. "Just a question of time," he said. "Bad shaking up," he said. "That's all it is." But he spoke to someone who was not there. "I'm not here any more," John said, but the doctor did not hear him. "I don't live here any more.")

"John," Barbara said. "Snap out of it! Listen to me—*snap out of it!*"

"I'm all right," he said. He spoke dully. It was as if he spoke to the road the lights brightened. "It was a mortar shell."

For a moment she was silent. There was a kind of tenseness about her silence; it was as if she snatched a moment of quiet in which to draw her thoughts together. Then she said, again, "John. Listen to me," and then, "Where have you gone, John?"

He did not answer immediately.

"You mean—what Father Higbee said?" she asked him, and spoke very carefully. "About this man who was with the Titus girl. The man she thought was—" She hesitated. "Was John Hayward?"

"I was talking about a real mortar shell," he said. "But—partly that. Yes. It was rather like one."

"He doesn't think it was you," she said. "He is quite certain it wasn't."

"In his own mind," John said. "The benefit of the doubt. And, he can't be sure it wasn't. Can't swear it wasn't." He spoke slowly, with long intervals between words. "How could he? He sees very little. The room was dark. It was months ago. If he testified, if he talked to the police, he'd have to say the girl told him that the man was John Hayward. He'd have to say the man wore what he called a 'showy' sports jacket—like the one the police will say they found in my apartment."

"Listen," she said. "Stop somewhere. Pull off somewhere. We can't talk this way. I can't hear half you say."

He drove a little way farther, pulled off where the shoulder widened. He cut the motor. He turned to face Barbara. He managed to smile at her, but at the same time he shook his head. He said it didn't, he was afraid, make much difference what they said. And, in spite of himself, he spoke from a distance, dully.

"He started it," she said. "Forced it. Insisted Julie introduce him as—as you. It was part of the plan."

"He," John said. "Yes, I suppose so, Barbara—I don't remember ever being there. At the inn. I mean before today."

"Remember?" she said. "What do you mean, remember? You never were." She waited. He merely looked at her. "What can I do with you?" she said, and there was a great anxiety in her voice. "Whatever can I do with you?"

"No," he said, in the same dull voice. "I was never there. I never saw the girl. I didn't kill her. I say that over and over, don't I?"

"Yes," she said. "Over and over. You needn't. I know. Do you hear me? *I know.*"

He touched her cheek with the knuckles of his loosely clenched right hand. He drew the knuckles down the softness of her cheek, and ran them, tenderly, along the slender, fragile bone of her jaw. She took the hand and held it, slim fingers twined around it.

"About the mortar shell," she said. "There was really a shell? In Korea?"

It had been in Korea, he told her. They had got, or nearly enough got, the range of his battery. A shell had exploded on it, or near enough on it. He had been buried, they told him. It was some time before they could dig him out. He had been unconscious for a time—they told him. He remembered opening his eyes in a field hospital, and of trying to answer a doctor who was talking to him.

"It was like being two people," he said. "One—still buried somewhere. Deep down. Trying to answer; thinking he had answered; not being heard. The other—the other somewhere else. Watching. As if from outside."

She merely nodded, and waited.

"Apparently," he said, "it was merely a bad concussion—oh, a few things cracked here and there, but nothing that worried them. I tried to explain afterward about being—well, in two parts—and they weren't particularly interested. Said there were all sorts of possible results from a concussion, and that I was lucky. Lucky and, after a couple of months, fit for duty. But then the whole thing stopped. With the armistice."

"John," she said. "Why did you remember that, just now? Why do you tell me about that? Just now?"

"I don't know," he said. "I just thought of it. Wondered if—" He did not finish. He looked at her. His eyes were no longer dull. He looked at her intently.

"All right," she said. "You wondered whether—how should I put it? Whether you ever came back together again? Whether one of these—these two people—could have lived a different life? John—do you really wonder that?"

He looked at her very carefully.

"Not when you say it," he said. "Perhaps—never. But there's a kind of shadow."

"I never," Barbara Phillips said, in a quiet voice, "heard anything so ridiculous in my life. Never in all my life." She looked at him; there was something like anger in her eyes. "You think I wouldn't know?" she asked him.

"I—" he said, and did not go on.

"Well?"

She waited for him to answer. He did not answer in words. He drew her to him. He kissed her lips and held his own on them, hard.

"All right," she said, when she could. "All *right*. Now let's go find this damn' tree by the tennis court."

"If we do," John said, "we'll find this other Hayward in the branches. Wearing a showy sports jacket."

"Now at that," Barbara said, "I wouldn't be surprised. I wouldn't be surprised at all."

He started the little car.

Detective Shapiro had talked to Miller. He had talked to Grady. He had talked to the desk sergeant at the barracks of Troop K, New York State Police. Miller—which probably would mean Grady—would talk to the police at Danbury, Connecticut, seeking co-operation. Shapiro had had a dinner, of sorts. Now he drove the small black sedan out of Brewster, and along a road he had followed before, and up a narrow winding road. Although things were going well enough, Shapiro felt dispirited. But I'm a sad man, he thought; everybody says so.

The chain across the Piermont driveway had been released. It lay, now, across the entrance to the drive. Shapiro found this interesting, and drove over the chain. When he had rounded a curve and so brought the house clearly in view, he discovered that there were several lights burning in it. Then he stopped the car abruptly, since a tall man had appeared in the headlight beam. The tall man carried a shotgun. Shapiro leaned out of the window and looked at the man, and the man came toward him, holding the shotgun ready.

"Going some place?" the man said. He was not, Shapiro decided, an amiable man. There were many unamiable people in the world, which was one of the causes of Detective Shapiro's sadness. "Mr. Piermont at home?" Shapiro said. He hoped the man knew how to handle shotguns.

"*Mister?*" the man said. "Ain't no mister, mister. Died thirty years ago. Thought everybody—" He stopped, apparently stricken by a new idea. "You trying to sell something?" he said. "If you are, we don't want it."

Unamiable people, and negative people—the world is full of them, Shapiro thought. He sighed at the thought.

"No," he said. "I'm a policeman. Is there a Mrs. Piermont?"

"What if there is?" the man said. But he lowered the gun to a position where, if he happened to pull the trigger, he would probably shoot off his own right foot.

"Couple of hours ago," Shapiro said, "there was a young couple. They talked to a man who was clipping trees."

"Pruning," the man said. "Talked to me. So?"

"I'm a policeman," Shapiro said.

He was told he had said that.

"What did they ask you?" he said. He was patient, as well as sad.

"About the Titus girl," the man said. "Is it any of your business?"

"Yes," Shapiro said. "I'm afraid it is. What did you tell them?"

"What you think? That she isn't here. In Florida, with the old lady." He paused; he moved a step closer. He asked Shapiro if he was sure he was a policeman. Shapiro said he was quite sure. He held out his badge. He flicked a lighter so the man could see the badge.

"Looks like it," the man said. "Well—seems she ain't. On account of, the old lady's here. Just came back alone." He looked at the badge again, very carefully. "Tell you," he said, "whyn't you go talk to the old lady? If it's about the girl?"

"That's a good idea," Shapiro said. "Why don't I?"

"Only maybe," the man said, "she don't want to talk to you. Cop or no cop."

"Maybe," Shapiro said. "Suppose I just drive—"

"Nope," the man said. "You stay here. I'll go ask her. If she wants to talk to you, she says so. See what I mean?"

"Yes," Shapiro said.

The man turned abruptly and walked up the drive. At the door of the house he waited for a minute or two, apparently for it to be opened. He went in. Almost immediately, he came out. He beckoned. Shapiro drove on up the drive. A tall old woman, who carried a cane and was dressed in a dark suit, stood at the door with the light behind her.

"You are prompt," she said, when he went up onto the porch. Her voice was very old, but it was also without quaver. It was a weathered voice, as her face was a weathered face. "I telephoned only twenty minutes ago."

She turned and went into the house. The man, who still carried the shotgun—if he pulled the trigger now he would get the left foot—motioned with his free hand. Shapiro followed the old woman into the house. He followed her into a living room. "Sit there," she said, and indicated a rocking chair. Shapiro, cautiously, sat in the rocking chair. His mother had had a rocking chair. She had been very proud of it.

"As I said," the old woman said, "you are very prompt."

"We try to be," Shapiro said. "Except—"

She waited. She had black eyes, very sharp in the ancient face.

"I'm a detective," Shapiro said. "From the city, Mrs. Piermont." He spoke the name with a slight question in his voice. She did not respond to the question. "Detective Shapiro," he said. "We are trying to trace a young woman."

"Certainly," she said. "Why did you think I telephoned? My ward. My former ward. Julie Titus. Why are you beating around the bush, Mr. Shapiro? Why won't you come to the point?"

The point seemed slightly elusive. He tried to come to it.

"Apparently," he said, "you called the police. I didn't know about that. I—"

"Don't," she said, "tell me you merely happened to be passing."

He was patient. He told her why he had come.

"Oh," she said, "Ebenezer told me about that. This young couple. Prying."

"Is Ebenezer—" Shapiro began, and was interrupted.

"The man you just talked to," she said. "Ebenezer Titus. He thought I was still in Florida. As if I didn't have any gumption. He's getting old, Ebenezer is. She's this girl that man killed, isn't she?"

"Your ward?" Shapiro said, and was asked, in a sharp voice, who he supposed she meant. "We don't know who killed her," Shapiro said. "But—we don't know, either, that she was Miss Titus. She was known by a different name."

"Evans," Mrs. Piermont told him. "Nora Evans. Why do

121

you think I came back? I explained all this to the officer I talked to."

"Yes," Shapiro said. "But—suppose you explain it to me, Mrs. Piermont. I don't like to trouble you, but—"

"Young man," she said, "I am quite in the possession of my faculties." There was an implication that Shapiro was not. "If you will listen," she said. He nodded; he listened.

She had been in Bradenton when she read of the murder of a girl named Nora Evans. "I always read about murders," she said. "I am interested in human nature."

"Oh," Shapiro said, and listened.

"The name," she said. "The address. She had written me from there using that name—Evans. Saying she was married. I suppose that was not true?"

"There's nothing to show she was," Shapiro said. "You knew there was a man? Before, I mean?"

She had, she pointed out, just told him. Certainly she knew there was a man.

"Not," she said, "that she was straightforward. I hoped I had taught her that, but no." And for a moment, he thought, the weathered voice seemed about to falter. It was reinforced. "However that may be," she said. "Many years in vain. But, what may we expect? Since she was ten—"

She told him, now with no apparent emotion, of her adoption—except that it was not legally adoption—of the girl Julie Titus; of the pretty, red-haired little girl of Briggs Hill. It was news to Shapiro. It was told briefly, but he did not, for the moment, ask more than an outline.

"I did what I could to protect her," Mrs. Piermont said. "It was not enough. In some fashion, she met this—this man. He persuaded her to desert me, without a word. Until, of course, some days later—then she wrote, saying she was sorry, and that she was going to be married. She hoped I would understand." She paused. "Understand," she repeated. She took a deep breath.

It had been inconvenient. She had expected the girl's companionship in Florida, as usual. The young were inconsiderate. One expected that. But—

The first letter had given no address. That had been in October.

"You made no effort to find her?"

She seemed surprised.

"I?" she said. "When she had, voluntarily, left me at a time she knew I wished her companionship?"

"Oh," Shapiro said.

It was after Mrs. Piermont had reached Florida—alone— that she had received the second letter. In it, the girl had said she was married, and had given the Eleventh Street address.

"I suppose," Shapiro said, gently, "that then she told you her married name?"

"Yes," the old woman said. "She said she was Mrs. Evans." She looked at him with doubt. "I fear," she said, "that you are very inattentive, Mr. Shapiro."

He said he was sorry.

"But," the old woman said, "if I wrote, I was to write her as Miss Nora Evans. The marriage was being kept secret. She did not say why. But now you tell me there was no marriage."

They knew of none, Shapiro told her. It was almost certain there had been none. She nodded to that. She told him that blood would tell. She paused for a long time.

"I may as well tell you," she said. "I was fond of the girl. I—I had great hopes for her. I had made plans for her. And— it was in a way of a test of something I, a good many years ago, believed in. That no blood was too bad—" She paused again. "She threw everything away. But—this does not interest you." Then, "She sent me a picture of this—this creature. Appearances are deceptive."

"You have this picture?" Shapiro asked her.

"Certainly," she said, and reached down to a black leather bag on the floor beside her chair. She opened the bag and took a photograph from it. It was a small print but it was clear enough—clear enough and unsurprising enough.

123

Shapiro looked at it. He nodded his head. Then he took the picture to a lamp and looked at it carefully.

"Well?" she said.

"It helps," he said. He went back to his rocking chair. "There was no identification of the body," he said, speaking as he was supposed to speak. "We'll have to ask you to make that identification if—" He paused. "If you feel equal to it," he said. "To be sure it is really the body of—was she a relative?"

"Oh," she said, "a Titus only. As I was. But—there is no real kinship. Nothing traceable. Long before the Revolution there were Tituses in these parts. There are many branches. Many kinds. Of course I will identify, Mr. Shapiro. Why else did I come back from Bradenton? Tomorrow, Ebenezer will drive me into the city. You will have the proper arrangements made?"

He would have the arrangements made, Detective Shapiro promised. He put the photograph in his pocket.

* * *

Everything had been thought of. Each hole was stopped. It came to that. For months—since at least the summer before —someone had worked carefully, foresightedly, so that now each avenue which seemed to present itself led only more deeply into the trap. And it was still not evident to John Hayward, walking slowly home after garaging the car, what the purpose had been—the central purpose. To trap John Hayward? To kill a red-haired pretty girl?

Driving back to the city through the spring night, they had stuck on that. (There had been no recurrence of the darkness of self-doubt, which was something—which was a great deal. As long as he was with Barbara—and now it seemed that she was walking with him, although he had left her at her father's house—he did not think that that would come back again.) There was a plot which they could not fathom. And, John thought, until we know the reason, we cannot hope to know the plotter. He turned it over and over in his tired mind. If, he thought, I could work out one of the things—even one. A simple thing.

He went into the small lobby of the apartment house he lived in. The adversary must have gone in and out of the same lobby several times. He must have gone through it, and up to John's apartment, and into it to get the laundry-marked shirts. He must have gone again to hang up the sports jacket —worn many times, no doubt, and certainly in the restaurant to which Father Higbee had taken them—to hang it in the closet, for the police to find and, as circumstances tightened the noose, make much of.

The adversary had a key. That was obvious. How he had got hold of it was not obvious. Nor was it obvious how he had, several times at any rate, got into and out of the apartment house unnoticed, by the elevator operators. There were only four apartments to the floor. If, several times, Harry or his alternate took a stranger to the same floor—the fifth—they might have become curious. At any rate, the adversary would have wanted to avoid—

Even before John went into the lobby, he had realized that he would have to wait for the elevator, which was not at the ground floor. Through the glass of the front door one could see the elevator door, and see it was closed. John had known this for years. Never before had he thought of it. The elevator car was trundling somewhere—and rather noisily—through the shaft. John would have to wait. Then, he would ask Harry if he remembered—

But another thought broke in. He thought of the fire stairs. The foot of the stairway was in sight from the elevator, so that the operator—in the car, or on his bench near the elevator gate—could see it. But not, evidently, when he had taken the car up with a passenger, or to get a passenger. So—

On impulse, to prove a self-evident point, John went to the staircase, opened the fire door, and climbed the cement stairs. So that part was easy, at least for a man vigorous enough to climb so many stair flights.

It was with the faint satisfaction of having proved something that John let himself into the apartment, and turned on the lights. He knew how the adversary had come in.

He found, and was annoyed to find, that he went into his own apartment tensed, as if to meet attack. But there was no attack. The apartment seemed empty. It took only seconds to find that it was as empty as it seemed. In the last few hours, at any rate, nothing new had happened—not here, within these familiar walls.

He remembered, then, that he had not looked in the hall closet. He opened the door—and found that, as he did so, he stood so that the door was, opening, between him and the closet. He swore, in exasperation, as he realized what he had done. If this went on, he thought, I'll be looking under beds. He turned on the closet light.

The boldly patterned sports jacket was gone.

You get punch drunk if it goes on long enough, John thought. The jacket had been there when he left in the morning. Now it was gone when he came home in the evening. Well—it was gone. Somebody had come and taken it. And about this, John thought, I feel nothing in particular. It is as if I had all along expected it to happen. He closed the closet door.

I'm damned if I'll even think about it, John Hayward thought. I'll think of one thing at a time. I'll think about that tree.

And then he bolted the apartment door. Whoever went in and out at will—the adversary; probably the police—would not come in tonight. John Hayward, numbly, poured himself a small nightcap, took one sip from it and put it on a table, and went into the bedroom and to bed. And almost at once he went to sleep.

He wakened at a little before eight. He knew where the tree was. It was as simple as that.

He showered and shaved. He made himself breakfast. He felt much better. His mind was rested. And there was more than that. In his mind, for the first time in many, many hours there was a kind of confidence.

He was smoking his first cigarette when the telephone rang.

"You're all right?" Barbara said. "You sound all right."

"Better," he told her. "A lot better. And—I've remembered about the tree. It's—" He told her where it was.

"I," Barbara said, "will be waiting on the curb."

Since it was not the cleaning woman's day, John washed the dishes. He went out, locking the apartment behind him—for what good that would do. He walked toward the elevator and when he was near, heard it rumbling in the shaft. He opened the door to the fire stairs and went down them.

In the stair well, he could hear the elevator moving in its shaft. So—that was the way the adversary had got out unnoticed. He went on down the stairs, listening. The elevator, which had gone up, went down again. He waited out of sight near the foot of the stairs. He could hear the elevator doors close and the car start up again. John went out of the apartment house, pleased with another point proved. It was a bright morning. He walked the two blocks to the garage. He ran the Corvette out into the sunshine.

Barbara Phillips was, quite literally, waiting at the curb. She wore a yellow suit, which somehow seemed the color of a spring morning.

They drove north into Westchester to find a tree by a tennis court.

X

GRADY RANG THE BELL. When it was not answered, he kept on ringing. Shapiro, who looked tired, and even more sad than usual, leaned against the wall. "Seems like he's not there," Grady said, with satisfaction, and Shapiro made agreeing sounds. Grady knocked on the apartment door and waited, and knocked again. Then he took a key out of his pocket and unlocked the door and they went in. Just inside, Grady, loudly, spoke John Hayward's name. He was not answered.

"Been here," Shapiro said. "Not long ago, either. Smoked a cigarette."

"The educated nose," Grady said. "Also, he slept here. Didn't make the bed. Tut. Tut."

Grady went to the hall closet and opened it. He said, "Uh-huh" and took the boldly patterned sports jacket off a hanger. He carried it back to a window and they looked at it. There was a rent in the back, and a small piece of the material was missing. Grady took an envelope out of his pocket, and fitted a small piece of colored wool where a piece was missing.

"Nice," Grady said. "Isn't it nice, Nate?"

"Fits," Shapiro said. "Everything fits, you notice."

"That's what makes it nice," Grady told him. He put the piece of cloth back in the envelope and the envelope in his pocket. He put the jacket over his arm.

"Anything else we want?" he said, and looked around.

Shapiro shook his head, sadly. They went out of Hayward's apartment, and locked the door after them. They went down the corridor to the elevator, and rang for it.

"You," Grady said to Harry, when Harry brought the car up. "When did Mr. Hayward come in last night?"

"Last night?" Harry said. "You want to know when he came in last night?"

"You're bright," Grady said. "Mr. Hayward. Last night."

"Far's I know," Harry said, "he didn't come in. Anyway, I didn't take him up."

"You were on all night?"

"Like always," Harry said. "On at nine. Supposed to go off at nine. And look what time it is."

Grady looked. It was nine-thirty.

"Like always," Harry said. "Comes when he wants to. Me, I stay till he comes."

"It's very tough," Grady said. "But you probably get some shut-eye."

"So if I do," Harry said. "They want to go up, they want to go down, they wake me up. Mr. Hayward didn't go up. *Or* down."

"All the same," Grady said, "he was in the apartment."

"Anyway," Shapiro said, "somebody was."

Harry didn't know about that. All he knew was— He'd told them what he knew.

"'Course," Harry said, "suppose he could have used the stairs. Don't know why he would."

"Maybe," Shapiro said, "he didn't want to wake you up."

At that, Harry laughed, with derision.

"Or maybe," Grady said, "he didn't want anybody to know what time he got in. *Or* went out."

"How," Harry said, "would I know? You want to go down?"

They went down. Harry stopped the car. "Mr. Hayward wear this coat much?" Grady asked, and lifted the arm with the jacket on it. Harry looked at it. He shook his head.

"Nice piece of merchandise," Harry said. "Like they say. No, I never saw him wear it."

"Sure you did," Grady said. "Must've."

"Listen," Harry said. "I know what I see."

"Just think about it," Grady said. "Must've seen him wearing it. It'll come back."

Harry shook his head.

"O.K.," Grady said. "When he comes in, call us. Here's the number." He gave Harry a card. "Going off," Harry said. "If he ever gets the lead out." He was told to pass the word along.

"Funny he don't remember," Shapiro said, in the police car, which was an unidentified black sedan.

"Lying," Grady said. "You know how these guys are, Nate. Figure they admit anything it puts them in a jam."

"Maybe," Shapiro said.

They drove three blocks to a garage. The Corvette they sought was not there. The space it occupied, on the ground floor, was shown them. Regulars like Mr. Hayward simply drove into allotted spaces. Easier all around. Late at night there was only one man on and he was usually upstairs washing cars. Last night's man was off by then, but he had a telephone. He was sleepy, but he answered it.

Probably the Corvette had been in during the night. It seemed, but dimly, that he remembered seeing it around seven in the morning, when he went across the street for a cup of coffee. But he couldn't swear to it. Maybe that was yesterday morning. What it came to, you got so you didn't notice.

"Nice convenient place to pick up a car if you wanted one," Grady told Shapiro.

"Where isn't?" Shapiro said.

The alarm went out—John Hayward, thirty-two, five-eleven, one hundred and sixty; light brown hair; probably driving a 1955 Corvette. Wanted for questioning *in re* suspected homicide.

***

It was a few minutes before eleven when John Hayward said, "This looks like it," and turned the Corvette onto a narrow, black-topped road, some distance above Katonah. The road skirted a lake. It was a pretty lake, set among hills. After a time, on the side away from the lake, there was the rolling green of a golf course, with golfers walking on it. Then, on the right, there was a dignified sign: "Carabec Country Club. Members only."

"Trespass," John told Barbara, and drove the car between

131

posts, into a parking lot in which there were half a dozen cars, and room for a hundred. He stopped with the bumper against a log barrier. They did not need to leave the car to see the courts—and to see, behind, bending above, the farthest court, a great maple tree, just coming into leaf.

"I must have been standing about there," John said, and pointed. "Whoever took the picture must have been about—" He hesitated. "There," he said, and again pointed. "Near the caddy house."

"You remember?" Barbara said.

"Not the picture," John said. "I mean, not anyone's taking it. The rest—yes, pretty much." He paused. "It's Hank Roberts's club," he said. "He brought me over. It was—it was the last week end in August, I think. It was hot as hell and—"

Roberts had made the suggestion at the office, Friday afternoon. It had been a dull, rather lazy, afternoon; an afternoon of marking time, waiting for the week end to begin. He and Hank Roberts had begun talking of tennis, starting, as he remembered, with discussion of the approaching national championships at Forest Hills. And Roberts had asked what he had on for the next day.

For the next day, John had had on only the Shipmans—a beach party in the evening at Southport, in Connecticut on the Sound. "Tell you what," Hank Roberts said, and told him what—he was to get up early, for once. On his way to Southport, he would drive to Lake Carabec and get in some tennis. There were some pretty good players who were always around on Saturdays. Hank would tell him how it was, and did. The same group played pretty much every week end; good group and good game. But it brightened things to get a new man in. And, after all, it was "more or less" on John's way to Southport.

John had agreed. He remembered it all quite clearly now, sitting in the car beside Barbara, looking at the tennis courts, and the tree which shadowed the farthest. On the court surface now there was only a splattering of leaf shadows. In August, the shade had been dense on half the court. Out of that heavy shade, tennis balls had seemed to leap, as if newly created. And into it, when one played that side, balls seemed to plunge, as the light was erased from them. But it was cooler in the shade.

"Oh," Barbara said. "That night. When we first—"

She did not finish, but took John's hand instead, and her slender fingers twined with his. It had not, at the Shipmans', on the beach at the Shipmans' club, been the first time she and John had met. Or perhaps, when one thought of it, it had been.

"I remember now," she said. "You said something about having been playing tennis. You started to say something about playing tennis and then—then you didn't go on with it."

(It had been warm on the beach. They had been in the water and had come out of it and were lying on the beach, a little way from the others. Their hands had touched, almost as if by accident. It had been their hands' first meeting.)

"I got here," John said, "about—oh, between ten-thirty and eleven. Hank had said ten, said they always started at ten. But I had a little trouble finding the place."

They had been finishing a set when John arrived—Hank Roberts and three other men, all much like Hank Roberts; all much like John Hayward. When the set was finished, Hank had taken him to the locker room and he had changed, and hung up the clothes he had been wearing in a locker. He could remember very clearly—there had been no lock on the locker. On lockers vacant for the use of guests there was never a lock. In a club it didn't matter. That was the theory, anyway. He had never had cause to question the theory.

He had got in a doubles game about eleven, or a little after, playing as Roberts's partner. "We won," he told Barbara. "Too easily. After that, we switched around."

The group had not been static. One man had been summoned to help take children to the beach; another had moved in. No one of them had played continuously; it had been pleasant, from time to time, to sit in the shade, sip at a beer—

slowly, since beer interferes with timing—and watch. It had been after one when they knocked off for lunch. Since they could eat outside, planned to play again after eating, they had not bothered to change. There had been six of them, in chairs on the lawn, around a table, eating sandwiches with a drink or two to wash food down. It had been lazy, relaxed. By that time he had been John to the others, except for one man who preferred Johnny.

"But," Barbara said, "you didn't really know them?"

Only Hank Roberts, really. If his life depended on it— He paused. "As," he said, "maybe it does." He was told not to be ridiculous. Well, then, if his life depended on it, he could not remember the names of any of the others. Not now. He could not remember their names or what they looked like, except that they looked like members of a club like Carabec.

The two were silent for a time, sitting in the small car, in the sun, trespassers at the Carabec Country Club, looking at a tree-shaded tennis court.

"Right about there," John said, and pointed again. "I would have been standing near the net post. Perhaps we were changing sides."

"But you don't remember anyone taking pictures?"

He did not.

"Mr. Roberts," she said. "Does he?"

"I don't know," John said. "I don't remember his ever making a point of it, anyway."

"But," she said, "he was around all the time. You played tennis with him. Had lunch with him—and those others?"

He hadn't, he said, made it clear. That was generally true. But in some of the sets, Roberts had not played. It was rather, John said, like being dummy at bridge. And, engrossed in the game, those who were not dummies paid little attention to the one—or to the two—who were. And—

He interrupted himself.

"Pit Woodson was around," he said. "Mentioning of bridge made me think of it. He was on the porch." He looked around at the club house. "There," he said, and pointed to the porch,

134

from which one could, if one chose, look out across the tennis courts. "Playing bridge, of course. And—Dick Still was one of those playing. I didn't know the others. I remember Pit saw me and gave a kind of salute and said something to Dick, and Dick did too. I wiggled my racket at them."

Later, as the tennis players were going back to it after lunch, he had said hello to Dick Still and Pit, who had not left the porch, but had lunched there. Pit had said something about the club, meaning the Harvard Club, being hopeless on Saturday afternoons in the summer and had suggested that, later, John might want to cut in. "Maybe," John said, not meaning a syllable of it.

"Most of the time, anyway," Barbara said, "Mr. Roberts was around?"

"Sure," John said, and then, "No. Wait. After lunch he said he had an errand to do, and that we had enough without him. Which we had. He came back just as we were knocking off—around four, maybe."

Then they had showered and changed. A little before five, John had driven across to Ridgefield and then down, through the rolling Connecticut hills, to Route 1 and off it, beyond Westport, to the pleasant village of Southport. (Carabec had not really been on his way.)

"While you—" Barbara began, and stopped. They watched a youngish man, dressed for golf, walk to a car and put his bags in it. He saw them. He waved heartily. They waved back. He got in the car and drove off.

"A big, happy family," Barbara said.

"He assumes we're members," John said, and was told, of course, they looked like members. Probably, Barbara said, it was crowded on week ends.

"It was that week end," John said.

"Members," she said. "Guests of members. And—what would prevent people like us, who look as if we might be members, merely walking in? So long as they didn't try to charge food or drinks?"

"I don't know there's anything," John said. "Except people don't."

She smiled at that. He caught the smile.

"All right," he said, "it's still true." He considered. "Generally," he said, and at that she smiled again, thinking that, slowly, he was learning—and thinking that, along with other things, he was very nice.

"If you mean, could anyone, club member or guest or plain outsider, walk in with a camera and take a picture of me," John said, "I'd say the answer is yes."

He looked at her, and his eyes narrowed a little.

"And," he said, "if you mean, could anyone have walked into the locker room and taken anything he wanted out of somebody's pockets—my pockets—the answer to that is yes, too. If he'd known which locker I was using."

"Mr. Roberts knew," she said.

"Actually," he said, "there aren't more than a dozen open lockers. Anybody, with time enough could find what he wanted. The tailors put buyers' names on labels in pockets," he said. "Usually. Anyway, mine does."

"And," she said, "your keys were in your pocket. Weren't they?" He nodded. "And you were here for hours. And anyone who wanted to could get your keys and have duplicates made somewhere—Katonah probably—and be back in—in how long, John?"

"An hour," he said. "Probably less than an hour."

"We're learning a little," she said. "Aren't we, John?"

He nodded. But he added that they were learning little that was more than a kind of filling in. The photograph could have been taken, the key abstracted and duplicated, by anyone—by Hank Roberts or Pit Woodson or Dick Still, certainly, but also by almost any man who looked like a country club member. And that this man did, they already knew.

"Well," she said, "we'll just have to ask some more people."

"I suppose," John said. He started the car. He backed it in a circle and headed out of the parking area. He turned right, toward Katonah, on the road which skirted Lake Carabec.

They had gone perhaps a mile when a siren sounded behind them—sounded imperiously. John pulled to the right, almost on the narrow shoulder, to let the demander pass. The State Police car passed—and turned in to block the Corvette. John stopped and a uniformed trooper got out of the car. He came toward the Corvette. He had a pleasant face, which displayed no animus. He looked, John thought, as if he might be planning to sell tickets to a policemen's ball.

"Mr. Hayward?" the trooper said. "Mr. John Hayward?" He was not selling tickets to a policemen's ball.

"Yes," John said.

"They want to talk to you," the trooper said, still pleasantly. "Like you to come along with us."

"Where?" John said.

"Hawthorne," the trooper said. "But we'll take you there, Mr. Hayward. You just come along and get in." There was still no animus in his voice. "The lady can take care of your car." He looked at Barbara Phillips. "That right, miss?" he said.

"Yes," she said. "But—"

"Listen," John said, "they've been all over it. Over it and over it."

"So?" the trooper said. "I wouldn't know, Mr. Hayward. Except, how could they? Whoever 'they' are? Because it only happened last night, didn't it?"

There was a long pause. Then John Hayward said, "What happened?" He could hear caution in his own voice, and a kind of apprehension.

"Mrs. Piermont got killed," the trooper said. "That's what they want to talk to you about, Mr. Hayward. Seems they think maybe you killed her."

He was still mild of voice; still noncommittal of voice. But then he said, "All right. Come along, Mr. Hayward," and his voice, although still there was no comment in it, was a policeman's official voice. "Come along and get in."

John Hayward went along and got in. They drove him to Hawthorne.

There they kept him waiting. He sat on a wooden bench, in the barracks of the State Police. A trooper sat beside him, waiting too. Finally, another trooper came to a door and said, "All right. You can come in now." It was rather as if John had sat in a dentist's reception room, waiting his turn.

He went into a bare room, with several chairs along one wall, and a table in the center. There were chairs at the table. Miller was in the room, and Grady, and a state trooper with sergeant's chevrons. "Well," Grady said, "here we are again, Mr. Hayward. What did you kill her for? An old lady like Mrs. Piermont?"

"Mrs. Piermont?" John said. "I didn't kill her."

"Didn't kill anybody," Grady said. "Makes it—"

"All right," Miller said. "Take it easy. It seems, Mr. Hayward, that you do know Mrs. Piermont's dead?"

"Yes," John said. "The trooper told me." He was careful again, watchful again.

"You were there yesterday," Miller said. "Asking about her. Why?"

"We—" John said.

"You and the girl," Miller said. "Yes, asking about Mrs. Piermont. And about the Titus girl. I suppose it was the only thing you could do, after Miss Phillips found the dress. Play along with her. Play innocent. Did you think if you killed Mrs. Piermont nobody could identify the Titus girl?"

"No," John said. "That would have been stupid, wouldn't it? Probably a dozen people could say Nora Evans was Julie Titus. If she was."

"So," Miller said, "you admit knowing she was. But I suppose you say you didn't know her, either. Didn't take her to the restaurant around here and bump into this preacher. Didn't get her to come to New York with you, and use another name, and shack up with her. Why the name change, Mr. Hayward?"

"I don't know," John said. "I don't know anything about it. I've been trying to find out."

Grady used, violently, a short, characterizing word.

"Take it easy," Miller told him. "Suppose you tell Mr. Hayward about this new one, sergeant. Since he doesn't know anything about it."

"Sure," the sergeant said. "Why not? It was this way, Mr. Hayward. 'Long about—"

Along about two o'clock that morning, or a little after two, Ebenezer Titus—yardman, occasional chauffeur, for Mrs. Piermont—had been awakened in his room over the garage. He had been awakened by the sound of a shot, coming from the house.

He had put on a pair of trousers and a pair of shoes, and had started toward the house, running. But he had heard the sound of other running feet and had turned in pursuit. Almost at once, however, he had changed his mind, deciding whoever was running already had too great a start. He had turned back toward the house, and had seen that the front door was open and that light was streaming through the door.

He had called Mrs. Piermont's name as he ran toward the house, and into it. Then he had stopped calling, seeing she could not hear. She lay sprawled in the hall, near the foot of the stairs, and her head was blown open. It didn't take a doctor to tell she was dead. He went around the body. He called the police.

It did not take much of a search to find the way the fleeing murderer had gone. He had run across a field and gone under a barbed wire fence—but not cleanly under the fence.

"O.K.," Miller said, and took a loosely wrapped package from the table and unwrapped it. He dangled a boldly patterned sports jacket from his big hands.

"Seen this before, haven't you, Mr. Hayward?" he said.

"Yes."

"Yours, isn't it?"

"No, it isn't mine. We've been over that."

"Show him, Grady," Miller said, and Grady took an envelope from his pocket, and strands of wool, in two colors, from the envelope.

139

"On a barb in the fence," Miller said. "Fits. See?" He showed the back of the coat, and a rent in the back. He said, "Well, Mr. Hayward?"

"When I got home last night, the jacket wasn't there," John said. "When I left this morning, it wasn't there. Where did you get it?"

"Tell him, Grady," Miller said. Grady told him.

"So you see how it is," Miller said. "Where were you at about two o'clock this morning, Mr. Hayward?"

"At home," John said. "In bed."

"Sure," Miller said. "About what time would you say you got home, Mr. Hayward?"

John thought. He guessed it at about eleven.

"Sure," Miller said. "Then you're all right. Out of it. All we've got to do is have the elevator man say what time he took you up, and that he didn't take you down again. That's right, isn't it?"

"No," John said. He spoke very slowly. "I walked up."

"Walked up?" Miller said, and his tone was full of innocent surprise. "Now how did you happen to do that, Mr. Hayward? Just tell us about walking up."

XI

SHE HAD FOUND again the little cluster of white houses, and the white church, in the hills near Brewster. She had not known whether she could find it; when she did come on it, she came as unexpectedly as they had come the day before. She pulled off the road in front of the rectory.

Father Higbee was in the garden at the side of the house. He was on his knees, bent very low toward the ground, peering at the ground. He wore what appeared to be old army trousers and shirt. Now and then, after examining it very carefully, he pulled a weed. From near by, Barbara spoke to him, spoke his name. He looked up at her and smiled benignly and it was clear he did not in the least recognize her. But he got up. He stood, smiling, a little rotund, rubbing his back.

"I was here yesterday," she said. "Barbara Phillips. With—"

"Of course," Father Higbee said. "Of course, of course. It's the wrong glasses again, I'm afraid." He moved close to her; he was only a little taller. Unexpectedly, he held out both hands to her. There was a good deal of earth on his hands, and they were stained green from weeds. She took them gladly. "My dear," he said, "there has been a sad thing—a very sad thing. Mrs. Piermont—we were talking of her only yesterday—"

"I know," she said. "That's the reason I've come back, Father. They think—" She stopped. "They've arrested John."

"My dear," he said. "My dear child." He rubbed his hands on his trousers. "Come," he said, "we'll have a cup of tea." He appeared about to pat her shoulder. He looked at his hand and shook his head.

They went into the white rectory, and into the room where they had talked the day before. He told her to sit down; that he would be only a moment. He went out and almost at once returned. "Margaret is making tea," he said.

"Father," she said, "when did it happen? When was she killed?"

"This morning," he said. "Very early, they say. I was not called. But—news spreads. It is not always accurate news, but it always spreads."

"Just when?" she said. "Do you know? And—how did it happen?"

"I think about two o'clock," he said. "Mrs. Kellems heard the police siren a little after that. It awakened her. Mrs. Kellems—" He paused. "There is little Mrs. Kellems does not hear," he added. "They say Angela apparently heard someone downstairs. Moving about. And went down. That would have been like Angela. She was—" He paused again. "A direct person," he said. "A courageous woman. She went down, I suppose, with her cane."

"Father—" Barbara said, and stopped. A small, spare woman in a house dress came in, carrying a large round tray. "Already had the water on," the woman said. She smiled at Barbara, and smiled sweetly. "There is nothing," she said, "like a good hot cup of tea." She put the tray down on Father Higbee's desk. "You ought," she told him, "to wash your hands, Father." He looked at his hands. "Indeed yes," he said, and began to pour tea. "Isn't that just like him?" the spare woman said, contentedly, and went out. "On the other hand," Father Higbee said, "it is clean dirt. And the vital juices of growing things. Drink your tea, my dear. Your boy will be all right."

"Why do you say that?" she asked him. "Everything's *wrong*, Father. Everything. You merely say that because—because it's the thing to say. Don't you?"

"You mean," he said, "because I am a clergyman, and therefore unctuous? No, my dear. I sat here with you and the boy." Somehow, John sounded very young; it was as if they were both children. "He would not kill an old woman," Father Higbee said. "Since he did not—"

"Innocence isn't enough," she said. "You know that. Even truth isn't enough."

"In the end," he said. "But you don't mean that, of course. Do drink your tea."

She drank. The tea was hot. It was strong. It seemed almost to reach a coldness in her.

"I realize," he said, "the importance of intelligence, my dear. Of—determination. You both have both. So, he will be all right. Have a piece of toast."

She shook her head.

Father Higbee reached into a drawer of his desk and took out a package of cigarettes. The package looked rather as if it had been sat on. He partially extracted two cigarettes and peered at them. He made a slight face at the cigarettes and then held the package toward her. She took a cigarette, and he took the other, and held a match across the desk, then to his own cigarette.

"Angela Piermont," he said, "was a wealthy woman. A very rich woman, by my standards. But in any case, wealthy."

She was puzzled.

"You mean," she said, "there might have been a lot of money in the house? That whoever killed her was only after money? Only a burglar?"

"I was not thinking of that," he said. "You may be right, of course. I was thinking—" He stopped and puffed at his cigarette. He seemed to nibble at it. "Julie would have inherited a great deal of money, again by my standards, if she had outlived Angela," he said. "Indeed, except for provision for Ebenezer Titus—he helped around the place, you know—she would have inherited all of it. I witnessed Angela's will. She invited me to read it. I—"

It had been almost a year ago. Mrs. Angela Piermont had, first, telephoned. Then, in a Rolls-Royce—a very elderly, very tall, Rolls-Royce, with Ebenezer Titus driving—she had appeared at the rectory. She had produced her will—a handwritten will, very short. She had asked Father Higbee to witness her signature, and that he call in Margaret Kellems —"my housekeeper, my dear"—as the other witness.

"I told her," Father Higbee said, "that I believed witnesses were unnecessary, since the will was a holograph. She said, 'Nonsense, man. Whatever gave you that idea?'

"Nevertheless," Father Higbee told Barbara, "I still believe I was right. But two more signatures could do not harm. All the money went to Julie, as I said. And—there was no provision for what was to happen if Julie died first. I pointed that out to Angela."

He had pointed it out. She had said, "Nonsense. She's a young girl. I'm an old woman." Father Higbee had reminded her that in the midst of life we are in death, regardless of age. He had been told that that was all very well to say, but not a thing any rational person believed. She had said, further, that it didn't matter to her. If Julie wasn't alive, "they could scramble for it."

"They?" Barbara said.

"Relatives," Father Higbee said. "Everyone has relatives. The rich have more than most." He put the cigarette, which had gone out, carefully on the edge of his desk. Almost at once, he knocked it to the floor with an elbow. "Now," he said, "they may be expected to appear. As Angela said, they will come out of cracks. She was—" He hesitated. "A forthright person. Perhaps not compassionate."

"Father Higbee," Barbara said. "Don't you see? Who are these relatives? Who gets the money?"

He smiled at her.

"Yes, my dear," he said. "I do see. Really I do. But I do not know who the relatives are. Or who inherits. Time will tell. I assure you, time will tell."

She looked at him. He nodded.

"They will be distant relatives," he said. "If they were close, I would have heard about them, I imagine. But—one will be closer than the others. So, one—or perhaps two or three—will inherit. A distant cousin, perhaps. The scent of money will draw them out."

144

"Father," Barbara said, "people kill for money. More often, probably, than for any other thing."

"Regrettably," Father Higbee said. "Most regrettably. Let me pour you another cup of tea."

* * *

So that was where they were, Shapiro thought, and stopped the black sedan some distance from the rectory. He could interview the preacher another time. It was a little surprising that the car had not already been picked up.

Since he had left Grady in New York and driven back to the country—and why he was the one who had to leave familiar streets for these odd open spaces he didn't know—Shapiro had been somewhat out of touch. He had been nosing around, as a guest of the county detective and the State Police. Detectives, even detectives first grade, are told only what they need to know. Now, inconspicuous in his inconspicuous car, he waited.

But when the girl came out of the rectory, Hayward was not with her. Possibly, Shapiro thought, they've tumbled to it. Perhaps he's hiding out. He looked thoughtfully at the rectory, at the same time putting the car in gear. If Hayward had decided to hole up, it seemed a little improbable that he would hole up with a clergyman. One never knew, of course. Damn' funny things could happen, in the country particularly. But following the girl looked like being the best bet.

He followed the Corvette. He followed it back through Katonah, and, at Bedford Hills, on to the Saw Mill River Parkway. The girl didn't seem to be in any great hurry, which was as well.

A Jaguar passed Shapiro, and then passed the Corvette. It did seem to be in a hurry. Well, Shapiro thought, he wasn't a traffic cop. Let the parkway police boys worry. He, nevertheless, noted the numbers on the Jaguar's license plate.

***

Miller was patient. He had been patient for upward of an hour. He was also reasonable—noticeably, carefully reasonable. He said, all right, if Mr. Hayward insisted, perhaps it had not been done to keep Mrs. Piermont from identifying the girl. He said perhaps they could think of a better reason. He said, suppose they started it from the dress. Suppose they put it this way—

John had not counted on the green dress. He'd got the labels off the other things. He had seen that the label already was off the green dress. "So did we," Miller said. "So that was one we couldn't check ourselves." He had not counted on Barbara Phillips's recognition of the green dress. Once she had remembered it, he had, of course, to play along. Play along to the shop in Danbury.

"I take it," John said, "you had us followed."

What, Miller wondered, did Mr. Hayward think they would do? Followed, and checked back on.

So, John and "this Phillips girl—bright girl it seems like she is"—had moved along to the Piermont house, and Mr. Hayward had put on a pretty good show. It hadn't happened, apparently, that he had previously bumped into this Eba—Ebenezer Titus. "Funny names people have in the country," Miller said. Anyway—

Mr. Hayward hadn't expected it to get that far. The whole point was it wasn't to get that far—that Nora Evans was to stay unidentified. He ought to have known that, by and large, people don't. But Mr. Hayward couldn't be expected to know that. When he and Miss Phillips got as far as the Piermont house, even if they didn't see Mrs. Piermont, the idea of keeping the girl's identity secret had to be given up.

"That's the way it was, wasn't it, Mr. Hayward?"

"No," John said. "I'd never heard of Mrs. Piermont. Of—any of it."

"Never heard of her," Grady said. "Never heard of Nora

Evans." He shook his head. "Seems like he don't get around much," Grady said to Miller.

Grady really hates me, Hayward thought. He's out to get me. With Miller it isn't personal, but he's out to get me too.

Miller was, he said, just trying to get things straight—trying to get the whole picture. The original plan was that nobody would ever get as far as the Piermont angle. Once they had, something had to be done about it. Miller would say for Mr. Hayward that he didn't give up easily. Of course, he could see Mr. Hayward's point. Identification of the girl wouldn't matter too much—maybe it wouldn't—if he could avoid a tie-in.

"So," Miller said, "you drive back to town and take Miss Phillips home. Then you drive back up to the country. To the Piermont place. You think the old lady is still in Florida. But, because this man Titus is around, you take a gun. Just on the chance you might need it. I don't say you went up there to kill anybody."

"That," John said, "is damn' nice of you."

There was no point in playing along, or pretending to play along. Miller did not appear to hear him.

"Before that, you've gone back to your place and gone up the stairs, so as not to let this elevator man see you. You get this jacket and—"

"Why?" John said. "Why would I want to wear the jacket?"

"We've wondered about that," Miller said. "Why did you? Didn't want to get your good clothes messed up, maybe? Or —because at night the jacket would show up dark? Not like the light suit you'd been wearing?"

"It's your story," John said. "None of it happened."

A squarely built man in civilian clothes came into the room. He nodded to Miller and Grady, and to the State Police sergeant. He sat down and listened.

"Oh," Miller said, "it happened, all right." He went on with it. John had gone back down the stairs in his apartment house, now wearing the jacket, which would show dark at night, and, Miller supposed, dark slacks. He had driven to the

Piermont place, found it dark, and got in—through a window; they had found the window—and started looking for what he had to find. Still not meaning to kill anybody, but with a gun along if he had to. Thinking the old lady was still in Florida. But the old lady wasn't. She heard him, and came downstairs.

"So," Miller said, "you used the gun. Why? Whyn't you just run?"

"You tell it," John said. "Maybe I just like to kill people."

"Tough guy," Grady said. "First a smart cooky. Now a tough guy."

Then, Miller said, still ignoring what Grady said, Mr. Hayward had run for it. Maybe he had seen Titus's light go on, in the room over the garage. Maybe, knowing somebody would come at the sound of the shot, he had merely run. He had come to a barbed-wire fence, and gone under it—and snagged the jacket. Wasn't that how it had happened? What was the point of denying it had happened that way?

"I don't know there's any point," John said. "But nothing like that happened. Somebody else owns the jacket—apparently wore it last night. Probably shot Mrs. Piermont. Put the jacket back in my place where you people found it this morning. It wasn't there when I left. Maybe whoever's doing this was waiting to see me leave and—"

"Oh God," Grady said. "Here we go again."

"You see what Grady means, Mr. Hayward," Miller said. "You see how it looks."

"All right," John said. "Why don't you charge me with it? You seem to think you have enough. I suppose you know what I was looking for? In the Piermont house?"

"Why sure," Miller said. "Sure we do. Something ties the whole picture together. Just a picture of you, Mr. Hayward. Just the picture Julie Titus sent back to the old lady, saying this was her new husband. Show him, Grady."

Grady showed him the photograph. It was a smaller print of the picture which had been in the Eleventh Street apartment. You could hardly make out the tree in the smaller print.

"So you killed the old lady for nothing," Miller said. "Yesterday afternoon, she gave the photograph to Shapiro. Told about how she got it in a letter from the girl—letter in which the girl said she was married and that this was a picture of her husband. So you went to all the trouble of killing her for nothing at all."

(Everywhere you turned, the hole was stopped. Always, the adversary had been before him. For minutes, while they watched him, John looked only, through darkness, at the top of a wooden table—seeing nothing, his mind dulled as if, repeatedly, but never quite crushingly, he had been subjected to numbing physical blows.)

"I don't suppose," Miller said, finally, "that you argue the picture isn't a picture of you? Or, that the old lady lied about how she got it? Of course, she's dead. But she told Shapiro. Or, maybe you think Shapiro lied? Maybe you think we're all lying."

John shook his head, slowly.

"The lie's bigger than that," he said. "It goes back further than that."

"Maybe," Grady said, "you got a twin brother you haven't told us about? Maybe he was shacking up with the girl? Maybe he was the one killed her?"

"Now," Miller said, "there's an idea for you, Mr. Hayward. Just come up with a twin brother."

The squarely built man got up and walked out. He had been, apparently, only a visitor. John was vaguely conscious that he had left. John sat shaking his head slowly. They didn't expect an answer.

"You see," Miller said, "the *girl* sent this picture of the man she called her husband. So you can't argue, as maybe you could about the one in the apartment, that somebody else put it there—that it wasn't there when she was alive. See what I mean? This one, she sent. You want to say the man was somebody else, and that this girl—this girl who was living with him—couldn't tell the difference? Or—or what?"

"Maybe," Grady said, "she was in it right along. She and

149

this guy work the whole thing out, so that she gets killed and it looks like Mr. Hayward killed her. How's that, Mr. Hayward? You like that one?"

John listened dully. (Everywhere you turned, the hole was stopped.) He put clenched fists to his forehead, and pressed hard. He tried to make himself think; tried to force consecutive thought into his swirling mind. And then—

"It could have been this way," John said. "This man offers to mail the letter. He goes out with it, and opens it, and takes out the picture she'd put in—the picture of him—and puts in this one of me. Addresses a new envelope and mails it."

His mind was suddenly entirely clear.

"Well, Mr. Grady," John Hayward said, "you like that one?"

Once more, Grady used his monosyllabic epithet. But Miller's eyes narrowed a little.

John looked at Miller's left hand.

"Doesn't your wife ever give you letters to mail?" John said.

"Oh," Miller said, "I don't say it isn't possible."

Grady made a noise. Miller did not look at him.

There was a sound at the door, and Miller looked that way. The square man who had left the room a few minutes before, stood in the doorway, and made a movement of his head. Miller got up and went to the door and the squarely built man said something. Miller beckoned Grady, then, and they both went out of the room, closing the door after them. The State Police sergeant, who remained in the room, went over and looked out a window. He said, "We need rain. My peas are drying up." He did not seem to expect an answer; getting none, he continued to look out the window at the spring afternoon.

For what seemed a long time, then, nothing happened— the sergeant continued to look out the window; John Hayward continued to look at the table top. Minutes passed, and the door opened and Grady came in. He looked at John with animus, and walked over and stood beside the trooper and looked out. Then the door opened again and Miller came through it. And Barbara was with him. For John, a kind of brightness came into the room with her.

He stood up. Before he could speak, Barbara came across the room to him. She was smiling, but there was a kind of intentness in her eyes. She walked into his arms and held her face up and he kissed her. She drew back.

"You're sweet," she said. "Sweet—and foolish." The words were light, spoken lightly. The voice was Barbara's, but she did not speak like Barbara. And the intentness remained in her eyes. Again he was about to speak, and again she spoke before him.

"Did you think I'd *let* you?" she said. "Did you *really* think that, darling? *To do a thing like that.* To tell them a—"

"Wait," Miller said. "Wait just a minute, Miss Phillips."

She turned to him, surprise and question apparent in her face.

"But—" Barbara said, and Miller said, again, "Wait just a minute, Miss Phillips. Mr. Hayward."

John waited.

"You told us," Miller said, "that you got home last night about eleven. Went up the stairs." Again John started to speak. "Never mind about the stairs," Miller said. "You said you got home about eleven. You agree you said that?"

John was sharply conscious, although he looked at Miller, that Barbara had turned back to face him. He felt, intensely, her being there, her looking at him. There was a kind of vibrancy about her, emanating from her.

"Of course," John said. "That's what I told you."

He did not, fully, know why he selected that word—said "what I 'told' you."

"John," Barbara said. "How—*foolish*. How sweet, but how *foolish!*"

"Miss Phillips," Miller said, "I keep asking you."

"But how can I?" Barbara said, and there seemed to be bewilderment in her voice. "Just stand here and let him—it's all so *ridiculous*."

(But it's not the way she talks, John thought. This—this hopping kind of speech.)

He looked at her. Her eyes spoke. For an instant, but only for an instant, his bewilderment continued. Then, as if it were a balloon pricked, bewilderment vanished.

"All right," John Hayward said, clearly, and, to his own ears, a little loudly, "I told you that."

"You stick to it? Or, do you want to change it?"

"Of course he wants to change it," Barbara said, speaking very quickly. "Of *course* he does. Don't you, John?"

He could feel them all around him waiting. Grady had turned from the window and was looking at him across the room. Then the sergeant turned, too. And Barbara looked up at him. It was as if her whole mind leaped the few physical feet between them. And, with his lips hardly moving, John smiled down at her.

"All right," he said. "I guess I made a mistake. I got the idea that—" He paused.

"Well?" Miller said. "What do you say now." He looked at John, then at Barbara Phillips.

"I was with Miss Phillips," John said. "I—I didn't want to drag her into it. It was late and—well—"

He hoped he was right. He was almost certain he was right. Then Barbara's eyes, although there was no apparent movement of the muscles around them, told him he was right.

"There," Barbara said. "Didn't I tell you? Why he thought —when we were just sitting in—" She seemed all confusion, this girl John had never really seen confused. She turned to John. By God, John thought, I'd swear she's blushing. How she—

"Sitting where, Mr. Hayward?" Miller said, and spoke very quickly, very sharply. "Where were you and Miss Phillips sitting at the time Mrs. Piermont was killed?" Just perceptibly, his voice underlined the word "sitting."

They waited again. Barbara did not try to speak. She's done all she can, John thought. And he spoke hurriedly. There was only one thing to say, and it had to be said in a certain fashion.

"In the library," he said. "In their house in the—" He stopped, as if he had caught himself protesting too much, bringing too many details to bolster a story. He hoped he did it well. Barbara's eyes were bright with the assurance he had done it well. Surely Grady, looking at her—surely Miller—would see that brightness in her eyes.

"You see?" Barbara said. "He thought you might—misunderstand. Think—what stodgy people—that is . . ." Again she seemed confused. "We were just sitting in the library," she said. "Talking about things. Trying to work things out. That's really all we—" And again she stopped.

(How, John wondered, can anybody—*anybody*—blush because they want to? He looked at Miller. And he saw that, as a little earlier—when he had himself suggested a possibility Miller could not dismiss—Miller's eyes narrowed.)

"And whatever you think," Barbara said, "we're engaged to be married and—" Once more she broke off. She moved to John's side, and took his hand in hers. And, through her hand, he could feel what he could not see—what none of those looking at her could see. Ever so slightly, Barbara was trembling.

"To protect you from this—implication," Miller said, and spoke slowly. "To make sure that no one would know you two were *sitting*—and *talking*—in the library at your father's house at two o'clock in the morning, Mr. Hayward was willing to take the risk of being charged with murder? Is that what you're saying, Miss Phillips?"

"It was foolish," Barbara said. "He knows that now. But—can't you see? It was—it was the sort of thing he'd do? Can't you see that? Because you might think—"

She stopped. This time, John thought, there was no calculation in the broken sentence. She stood quiet by John's side, and Miller looked at both of them.

"You expect us to believe this?" Miller said. "You both expect that?"

It was John who answered.

"I don't see what else you can do," John said. "Do you?"

John looked blandly at Miller. Then he turned his head and looked at Grady. Grady was very red in the face. John knew the word he wanted to use, and couldn't use with Barbara there. For an instant, John felt almost sorry for Detective Grady.

"And I suppose now," Miller said, "you both think we say sorry, and that you can go along?"

"No," John said. "I don't suppose you go that far."

"No," Miller said. "We don't go that far. We're not sorry. We think you killed them both, Mr. Hayward. But—you can go along." They looked at him. They looked at him in astonishment. "For now," Miller said. "Just for now. And—don't bother to go too far, Mr. Hayward. Don't plan to go far at all."

After the State Police sergeant had taken them out, Miller stood for some seconds looking at the door. Then he turned and looked at Detective Grady.

"Did you," Miller enquired, his voice heavy with imposed forbearance, "ever hear of a search warrant? You know—you go to a judge and you tell him things, and he signs a piece of paper. Ever hear of that?"

Grady did not say anything. He was very red of face.

"Because," Miller said, "you do things that way, and you've got something. Something we can use. You use one of your pet keys and go into a guy's apartment and take what you want—like a sports jacket with a hole in it—and where are you, Grady? Because the guy gets a lawyer. You know—l-a-w-y-e-r? And the lawyer says your evidence was illegally obtained. And the judge says it sure was. And where do you go then, Grady? Out on your tail is where you go."

Grady still did not say anything.

"And then the guy turns up with an alibi, Grady," Miller said. "Just to make it harder. A nice clean alibi."

"They're lying," Grady said.

"Sure they're lying," Miller said. "And the girl is important people, Grady. And he went to Harvard and works in a bank

—very nice important job in a nice important bank. And the jury looks at the pretty, important girl and the nice clean-cut young man who went to Harvard and—what, Grady?"

"They're lying," Grady said, again. "Are we supposed to let them get away with it?"

Miller was a man who suffered much. He shook his head, slowly, to show how much he suffered.

XII

JOHN DROVE THE Corvette around Hawthorne Circle and headed toward New York down the Saw Mill River Parkway.

"They know we're lying," John said, with the car headed south, moving at the stipulated forty miles an hour.

Barbara had been very quiet since they had left the barracks. Now she nodded. But then she turned to him. She grinned suddenly.

"I hope," she said, "they think only half of it was a lie. The part about—what we were doing."

"When your father hears of that," John said. "Just wait until he hears of that!"

"My father," Barbara told him, "is a man of wisdom. Also, quick on the uptake. You weren't so bad yourself, come down to it."

She had, John told her, what are known as speaking eyes. All he had done was listen.

(For this moment, Barbara thought, we almost match the car, are almost what we look to be. This is seemly. But then she saw the smile on John's lips at first become fixed there, as if forgotten, and then vanish. He looked very drawn, very tired.)

"It's only a reprieve," John said. "Sooner or later, they'll pick me up again. Harder next time. They'll—" He paused. He looked only at the road, with bleak eyes. "Townsend was up when we got there," he said. "He knows when it was. He knows I didn't go in with you."

"The trouble with being a banker's daughter," Barbara said, "is butlers. I grant you that."

He smiled faintly, but did not take his eyes from the road.

"Actually," she said, "it was more than the alibi. I overheard them talking. After I'd said we were together. Miller and the man who got so red in the face—"

"Grady," John told her abstractedly.

"—and another man—a square sort of man, who seemed to belong to the State Police, not the city police. He said, 'Now, Miller. If you want to, naturally. We don't. Not on the kind of evidence you've got.' Grady said something I couldn't hear. The square man said, 'You can't take the jacket into court. Because, you're not supposed to have the jacket. And, on this one, the jacket's all you've got.'"

John nodded.

"John," Barbara said. "I've found out some things. One thing, really, but other things seem to grow out of it. Stop some place so—wait. Have you had anything to eat?"

"No," he said.

"So we can talk, then," she said. "The place by the lake."

❋ ❋ ❋

Shapiro had told Miller what had been found out—from Ebenezer Titus, from Mrs. Piermont's "local" lawyer in Brewster, from the bank in Brewster. Most of it had been found out by the State Police, and by men from the county detective's office, and by an assistant district attorney from Carmel. For the most part, Shapiro had gone along to listen. Shapiro gave details without comment; watching Miller's face. When he told Miller about the will which had been found in Mrs. Piermont's desk, Shapiro was interested to notice that Miller's eyes narrowed.

"And you followed the girl from this preacher's place?" Miller said, and was told that that was right. "Find out what she wanted there?"

Mildly, Shapiro pointed out the obvious—that if he had stayed to ask the preacher what the girl wanted, he would have lost the girl. He had thought the girl might lead him to the man. He didn't know they already had the man.

"All right," Miller said. "I'll take Grady back with me. You come along after us. Let them work this one out, seeing they're so keen on regulations." He paused, briefly. "Not that you and Grady didn't pull a prize one," he said. Shapiro could have told him that that idea had been Grady's. Shapiro did not. He merely looked sadder than before. He went to the washroom.

When he came out, Miller and Grady were gone. He started past the booking desk to the door, and the sergeant said, into a telephone, "That's right, sir," replaced the receiver and said, "Hey. You." Shapiro walked over, his face sad.

"Hayward's lawyer," the sergeant said, indicating the telephone. "Heard we had his man locked up. Was all set to come out and unlock him. I told him he needn't bother."

"All right," Shapiro said.

"Told him we merely wanted Mr. Hayward to clear up a couple of points," the sergeant said. "That after he had, we turned him loose. All in nice smooth talk, of course."

"All right," Shapiro said.

"A man named Still," the sergeant said. "Richard Still. That the right man?"

"Yes," Shapiro said. "That's—" He stopped. "Only thing," he said, "is how he knew we had Hayward here?" He stopped again. "Probably," he said, "the girl called him. Hayward didn't call himself?"

He had not, that the sergeant knew of.

Shapiro started on again. Near the door, he stopped and looked, as if in reproach, at a telephone booth. He sighed deeply, went back to the desk, and borrowed the Manhattan telephone book. He noted a number down and went back to the booth and called the number.

"Laughton, Murphy and Wahlstein good afternoon," a girl said, purring slightly. Shapiro asked for Mr. Still—Mr. Richard Still. "One moment please," the girl said, still purring.

He waited the moment. Another voice, still purring, still female, said, "Laughton, Murphy and Wahlstein Miss Norby speaking."

"Mr. Still?" Shapiro said, with patience.

"I'm very sorry Mr. Still is out of town. Will anyone else do?" Miss Norby said.

Shapiro said, conventionally, "Um-m." Then he said, "Could you give me a number where I could reach him?"

"I'm very sorry I'm afraid I do not have a number for Mr. Still," Miss Norby said. "Can someone else help you?"

Nobody could. Shapiro replaced the receiver and for some seconds looked at the wall telephone, without seeing it. Perhaps Miss Phillips had called before Mr. Still went out of town. Or, perhaps, since she was a very important young woman, she had received special treatment, information mixed with purring. Perhaps Mr. Still's out-of-town trip had taken him into Westchester and Putnam counties and he had, in some fashion, acquired information on his own.

And perhaps, of course, it had not been Mr. Still at all, but someone else who was keeping track of John Hayward.

Well, Shapiro thought, perhaps it's been too easy all along. He wondered if Miller had begun to think that too. Then he thought of Grady, and shook his head and sighed. He left the booth and the barracks, and drove the black sedan toward New York on the Saw Mill River Parkway.

Just south of the circle, he was passed by a Jaguar. You did, Shapiro thought, see more and more of those foreign cars. He noted the numbers of the Jaguar's license plate. Or, he thought, I seem to see a good deal of one of them. Not that it meant anything. But he picked up speed somewhat, so that—unless, of course, the Jaguar got in a hurry—he could keep the low, deep-throated car in sight.

***

It gave them, Barbara said, a logical explanation. It gave them things you could add together, so that you came up with a sum. It brought things into order, however bizarre the order. You could start with a premise, and build on that. "As," she said, "you like to do," and then, quickly, "As everyone likes to do."

They sat at a table by a window, overlooking a lake. There were two swans on the lake. They were, she thought, very

160

pompous swans. They had been too late for lunch; not too late for a drink, for sandwiches, for coffee. They sat, now, over coffee. She had told him about the will.

"Which," he said, as they went over it again, pinning it down, "now means nothing, if Father Higbee is right. It would be, I suppose, as if she had died intestate. We'll have to ask a lawyer—if they give us time."

If Mrs. Piermont had died intestate, the surrogate's court would take over. Relatives would present claims to the court; in time, the nearest, if one was clearly that, would inherit. "In the event of a tie," Barbara said, "the prize will be divided equally." And—final adjudication would take a long time. It always did. And that was part of it—part of the plan. They agreed on that. "Granting the premise," John said. "Always granting the premise."

But John had changed, Barbara saw, and was glad. He looked tired no longer. It had been he, once they had started, who had done most to work it out—to backtrack on a plan which rested, in some part, on the slowness of procedure in surrogate's courts everywhere.

The man—"I've come to calling him the adversary," John said. "To thinking of him as that"—had reason to know that, while distant in kinship from Angela Piermont, he was still nearer than others. Family records, presumably, had told him that. He knew, certainly, that Mrs. Piermont was wealthy. He decided to inherit her money. And—Julie Titus stood in his way.

It was to be presumed he had found this out from the girl herself, during a kind of preliminary survey. He had been careful from the start. He had, presumably, arranged to meet Julie by apparent accident. It would not be hard in the country, if the girl took walks, if the man—the adversary—were patient. It should not have been difficult for him to advance the relationship with the girl to the point of confidence.

"The poor thing," Barbara said. "Cooped up, fenced in, like—like a kitten in a cage. And, we know he's outwardly attractive, good-looking." John raised his eyebrows. "He looks like you," she said. "Enough, at any rate. A type Americanus. Or—Harvardianus."

John had said "all right" to that.

The money went to the girl. He—the adversary—found that out. So, the thing was to kill the girl. Then, before Mrs. Piermont changed her will, to kill Mrs. Piermont. And then, merely to wait. In her first development of her theory, when she was bright with it, excited with it, Barbara had hesitated there and some of the brightness faded. "All the rest of it," she said. "Involving you. It seems such a long way around. So—so improbably long a way around."

And then John had thought a moment, and shaken his head.

Once the improbability of murder was accepted—accepted and then disregarded because murder had been done—the length of the way around could be understood. He went over that, speaking slowly—once holding, halfway to his mouth, a piece of sandwich, and holding it there, forgotten, for minutes, and putting it down again untasted.

The purpose was to get the money. But, there is always a basic difficulty in murder for gain—the one who gains is the first choice as the one who murders. Unless—an alternative murderer is provided, neatly trussed and on a platter. Once the alternate is tried and convicted and put to death, the way is reasonably clear. The police may be trusted to wash their hands of that one.

"It's there the slowness of surrogate procedure comes in," John said. "It takes a long time, in this country, in this state, to get a murderer executed. But—it takes a longer time to get the surrogate's proceedings over with. One case the bank was concerned with, it took four years and about ten months. There'd be time enough for the alternate to go to the chair." He looked out the window at the pompous swans. "The alternate in this case," he said, "being me. Why? A kind of eeny-meeny-miney-mo?"

They decided that, among those who met certain basic qualifications, it might well have come to that. The man chosen needed to be of a certain physical type. It was desirable that he live alone and be unmarried. It would help—although under the circumstances it was not essential—if some motive other than passionate violence could be adduced against him. It was necessary that he be a man on whom the adversary could, to some degree, keep an eye. The whole scheme fell apart if, for example, the man chosen as—as "fall guy"—happened to be in San Francisco on the day of the murder, and able to prove it.

There did not have, they agreed, to be any real identity of appearance, but only the most general of similarities. Suggestion would do the rest, and the inability of the average person to remember faces. One read often of mistaken identifications, and there were, quite probably, many others of which one did not read, because the police had not been taken in themselves. General type resemblance would have proved adequate—had proved adequate. Of course, the adversary could not appear as, in this case, John Hayward among people to whom John was well known. But that had been easy to arrange.

"A type," John said. "A man about whom nothing is outstanding. In other words, again, me." He smiled faintly at his girl. "Come down to it," he said, "I don't sound like much, do I?"

"In the eye of the beholder," Barbara said. "Me. Yes. Of course, I'm prejudiced. For some reason."

"Why?" he asked, and was told that there was no time to go into that.

"Some day," she said, "I'll write you a memo. 'From the desk of Barbara Hayward. To—dear John. Subject: Why you sound like much.' Meanwhile—"

Meanwhile—who?

To make it easy—if "easy" was the word for any of it—they would assume that the adversary had been at the country club that day, and not as a casual trespasser. Assume, also, that he had been at the Harvard Club at lunchtime on the previous Saturday. They came up with?

"Hank Roberts," he said. "Dick Still. Pit Woodson. Possibly, Al Curtis. I didn't see him at the Carabec Club, but he might have been there."

"Somebody," she said, "who takes pictures. And—knew you would be at the club that day."

To the first, he agreed, but pointed out that almost everybody did, or could. There had been nothing about the photograph that anybody, armed with the simplest camera, and a little luck, might not have achieved. But, as to knowing that he would be at the club—

"One of the things we've got to remember," he said, "is that there wasn't, at any given time, any great urgency. Up, I mean, to the moment of killing the girl. He allowed himself months, and he didn't have to do anything any particular day. He could just—mosey around. Like—like a kid picking up odds and ends, a board here and a piece of iron pipe there, to make a shack. The kind of shack depending on what was around to be picked up. He didn't *have* to have a picture of me. He didn't have to have the girl introduce him to Father Higbee as me. He had time enough to be an opportunist. If it hadn't been one thing, it could have been another."

He had, she said, to have access to John's signature, since he had forged it. Could they get anywhere with that?

John thought. He shook his head. Hank Roberts had any number of opportunities to study his signature. He vaguely remembered he had bought something from Curtis, and given him a check for it. He had had, for the bank, some correspondence with the law firm Still worked for. He stopped.

"Mr. Woodson?" she said. "He's just a name to me."

John couldn't remember any opportunity Pit Woodson would have had to study his signature. Unless—

"I've got a vague recollection of giving him a check once," he said. "Settling my share of bridge losses, I think it was. I can't be sure, though."

It was all shadowy—shadowy to her, too familiar to him to have features. But that, of course, was part of it. The adversary was himself a man quite ordinary in appearance, and apparently in habit.

An ordinary man, capable of quite out of the ordinary behavior. And—quite extraordinary ability to plan ahead; to contrive, step by step, toward a goal kept always in sight. A chess player. Did John know whether any of them played chess?

"Hank does," John said. "I'm told he's good at it. But—it isn't much, is it?"

"All the same," she said, "it's there some place. What can be raveled up can be unraveled. Mr. Woodson doesn't play anything but bridge?"

"Pit?" he said. "I shouldn't think so. Not old Pit." He looked at his watch. It was after four. They might, he supposed, be getting along. "Grady won't know where I am," he said. "Make him fit to be tied."

They got up. Back in the little car, they drove through the afternoon toward the city.

"Does one of them need money?" Barbara said, after for some time neither had said anything.

He thought they were all reasonably solvent. Except, possibly, Al Curtis. He didn't know about Al. A few weeks before Curtis had left the company he'd been with for about a year. Probably, however, because he'd come on something better.

"Like," Barbara said, "a lot of money?"

He had no answer to that. Anything was possible. That was precisely the trouble. Anything at all was possible.

* * *

The Jaguar had got in a hurry; Jaguars almost always did, sooner or later. Shapiro had made no special effort to keep up; his interest in the Jaguar was idle, based on the coincidence of having seen it at least once, and perhaps more than once, before. Determined pursuit of it would have been a wild-goose chase, and Shapiro could not encourage himself to chase wild geese. It would not be thought well of. But, all the same, he was now engaged in what was probably a similar pursuit.

The chances were a good many to one that Grady was right. Shapiro was not particularly fond of Grady, but that had nothing to do with the fact that Grady was right more often than not. This one was probably as open and shut as Grady, and presumably Miller (although one could never be entirely sure about Miller) thought it to be. All the same—

All the same, Shapiro was in the genealogical section of the New York Public Library, which was not where he was supposed to be. He was supposed to be back in the squadroom at the precinct, not in pursuit of the wild goose—or the wild Titus. He was not supposed to be satisfying, or as it now turned out not satisfying, an almost unmotivated curiosity. It was almost certain that Hayward was lying, and had tricked the girl into lying for him. That was too bad; she seemed a nice girl.

But the matter of the will did make one think; did arouse curiosity. Somebody was going to get a substantial sum of money, now that the Titus girl and Mrs. Piermont were both dead. That someone would be, in some fashion, a Titus, but almost certainly not named Titus. It was not going to be that easy.

The genealogical section was a large room, with card indices, an attended counter, and several long tables with heavy wooden chairs. Some of the chairs were occupied, largely by men who, if not actually wearing beards, gave a generally bearded impression. Although a library man in his spare time, which was inconsiderable, Shapiro had not before been in this section. He did not need to know who his own relatives were. Even less did he need further information about the relatives of his wife. About them, Shapiro thought sadly, but without animus, he already knew enough.

He looked up Titus in the card index and realized at once that he was not, in the short time he could allow, going to be able to satisfy his curiosity. There were too many Tituses, and too much had been written about them—they appeared in

166

standard reference books, and in privately printed books (which would, he thought, be small and badly printed and yellowed with years) and in pamphlets. There was *The Titus Family in the United States* and *The Tituses of Rockland County, New York* and *Descendants of Rufus Titus, Gent.* (That had been published in 1824 and could be presumed to leave things more or less in mid-air.) There were, also, innumerable cross-references.

Shapiro made out a slip for *The Tituses of Rockland County, New York,* which seemed as large a nibble as he had time for, and handed it in. He waited, patiently, in the chair assigned, in front of a number on the surface of a table. After he had waited for some time he went to the counter and asked.

"I'm afraid—" a trim woman of middle age, with neat white hair, began and a pneumatic tube popped. She opened the container and looked at its contents and shook her head. "*The Tituses of Rockland County,*" she said, "cannot be located. I'm very sorry."

"In use?" Shapiro said. "In the bindery?"

"They are making a search," she said.

"Then," he said, "it isn't in use? Or in the bindery?"

"Well," she said, "it's got to be somewhere, hasn't it? But—" He waited.

"I am afraid," she said, "that it has been misplaced. Temporarily, of course. Of course, only temporarily."

"Can you tell whether it's a large book?" Shapiro asked.

"I don't—" she said and was told, sadly, that it was rather important. She looked again at the slip he had written, which was now returned, annotated. She said, "Oh! Police Department."

Shapiro nodded, dolefully. She went to the card catalogue, then. She found the card. She said it was quite a small book.

"About," Shapiro said, "pocket size?"

"Oh," she said, "it would quite easily go into a man's pocket. Or a woman's bag. But the people who come here never—"

"Of course not," Shapiro said.

"And anyway," she said, "the slips are kept on file and it would be easy to find out who consulted it last. The name, you know."

"Yes," Shapiro said, and his voice was more than ever sad. "There'll be a name on the slip." He paused. There wouldn't be time for that. The radio in the car was already, beyond doubt, talking, with increasing asperity, to an empty seat. He said he would be back, or someone would.

If by any chance Hayward wasn't lying, and there was another man, the other man was getting around.

Shapiro walked down the wide marble stairs from the third floor of the library.

The man (who probably didn't exist) had already got around a lot. And—mightn't he be thinking he still hadn't got around enough, if Hayward was still not charged with murder? And—mightn't he try to get around a little more? In his place, Shapiro thought, I think I might. I think I know where I'd go next.

* * *

"At six-thirty, then," Barbara said, and slid out of the little car. On the sidewalk, she turned. Her face was very serious and her eyes were wide. "You won't be late?" she said. He smiled, not too successfully. The intentness of her expression did not change.

"No," he said. "Not unless they decide to pick me up."

He watched her go quickly up the stairs to the front door of the house; watched the door open; Townsend always on hand to open doors; Townsend, always loyal. He hoped that Townsend's loyalty could be so far extended. She would not, they had agreed, ask too much. False testimony under oath would not be requested. They could only ask for time—only ask that, for the time, if questioned, Townsend would forget that Miss Phillips had come in the previous night before eleven and come in alone, and that afterward he had heard nothing of a visitor.

Although what, John thought, driving the little car away, they would do with the time was a question. He agreed they could not merely sit and wait—and that they could not be apart. That last was what it came to, whatever they said—however they agreed that two heads were better than one; that they would think of something; that there must be some way the two of them, working together, could find out. What it came to was more simple. They could not, now, be apart. When they were apart, there was nothing. They had not needed to say this, or even to hint at it. Already, driving away, he was swept by loneliness.

She would see Townsend and see what she could do with Townsend. She would change. He would garage the Corvette, since a car in town was only a nuisance, and "freshen up" and then go back for her. That was the plan.

＊

"Oh, Townsend," she said, when he let her in. "There's—" But she stopped with that. Her father was sitting in the library, the door open to the hall. "Nothing important," she told Townsend. "Later." He said, "Yes, miss," and she went into the library. Her father stood up and looked down at her. He said, "Well, Barbara?"

"Not very," she said. "Not well at all, father."

She sat down and, after regarding her for a moment, he, too, sat. He indicated a highball on the table beside him and raised eyebrows.

"No," she said, "I'm going out again."

"With Hayward?" he said. "But I suppose that is a needless question."

"With John," she said. "Father, things are worse for us." He waited. She told him why. Then, he handed her a newspaper —a late edition of the *World Telegram and Sun*.

It was on the front page. The headline read, "Aged Recluse

Slain." The "recluse" was Angela Piermont, who was also "wealthy" and "Social Register." The death was being investigated by the State Police and the county detective's office and—"it was learned that city police have been called in to co-operate in the investigation. Deputy Chief Inspector Artemus O'Malley would neither confirm nor deny that the killing of Mrs. Piermont may be connected with the slaying Saturday afternoon of the beautiful red-haired girl who lived in East Eleventh Street under the name of Nora Evans."

She handed the newspaper back. She said, "They questioned John. Then—they let him go. Partly because—" She paused. "I said he was here with me, father," she said.

He looked at her steadily; there was slow thoughtfulness the way he looked at her.

"I take it," he said, "that that is not true?"

"No," she said. "That is not true."

"And," he said, "that Townsend knows it isn't?"

"Yes," she said. "You see things, don't you?"

"When they concern you," he said. "Do you think it would be fair to Townsend to ask what I suppose you plan to ask? Since he might not feel free to refuse?"

"I've known him," she said, "since I was a little girl. A girl so high."

"All the more reason," Martin Phillips said. "Don't you think so?"

She did not reply.

"It occurs to me," he said, "that it has been some time since Townsend has had a holiday. It would be only a palliative but—perhaps a week?"

"You think of things, too," she said. "A week would help. Only—"

"Oh," Phillips said, "starting at once. This evening. You are still very sure, Barbara?"

"Very sure," she said.

He nodded. He sipped his drink. She started to stand up.

"The bank," he said, "handled Mrs. Piermont's investments. I remembered when I saw her name. Some of them, at any rate. Her investments were considerable."

Barbara sat down again. She leaned forward a little in her chair.

"I don't know that it has bearing," he said. "Or what bearing it could have. And, everything seems to be in order."

"You—what?" she said. "Had someone check up?" She closed her eyes. She took a deep breath. She said, "John?"

"No," he said, "not your John, my dear. Henry Roberts was her advisor. But everything is entirely in order."

"He might have gone up—I mean to her house—to see her? To talk about her investments?"

"Oh," her father said. "Probably he did."

"The girl lived there," Barbara said. "The girl who was killed. Her name was really Julie. Julie Titus. She met a man who pretended to be John. She—she might have met Mr. Roberts."

"Perhaps," he said. "We have confidence in Roberts. But that goes without saying." He lighted a cigar, taking time with it. "Roberts was not at the bank this afternoon," he said, when the cigar was drawing. "He was representing us in—certain preliminary negotiations. So I had no opportunity to ask."

"To—" she said. "You would have asked? To—help John?"

"Hayward," her father said, with great gentleness, "seems to have become entangled in my life."

It was almost six when Barbara went up the stairs to her rooms on the third floor. As she stood in the shower, water beating against the rubber cap tight on her small head, the rushing water seemed to be talking—seemed to be saying, over and over, "Roberts. Roberts. Roberts." After the water had stopped, as she toweled hard, as she dressed, the name still repeated itself over and over in her mind. If Roberts had met the girl—if—if— *A place to start*, she thought. An end of the knotted string—surely this would be the place to start. Surely—

She was very quick. But it seemed she could not be quick

enough. Although there was no need to hurry, she hurried so that, when she was putting lipstick on, her hand trembled for a moment. She made herself be slow, then—slow and careful. Very delicately she touched off lipstick which had gone astray. Very carefully she retraced the curving line. But she was still ready by twenty after six and then she stood at the front door, waiting. She stood so she could look up the street, toward the west—look for the cab which would bring John back.

For a time there were no cabs. Then several came and she leaned forward toward the door and put her hand out toward the knob which would open it. But none of the cabs slowed, pulled in to the curb. Another cab turned in at the corner and came through the street—and *slowed*—and then went on again and finally stopped across the street. A woman got out. She had a poodle on a leash. Then there was another cab, but it was empty. And another—but— And another.

At six-thirty-five she had her slim hands clenched into fists. She could feel her heart beating rapidly—too rapidly. She took a deep breath, but the exciting beating of her heart did not slow. A cab turned in at the corner, and she found that she was holding her breath. But the cab went on.

She tried to steady—to quieten—her mind, which seemed somehow to be beating with her racing heart. Six-thirty does not mean six-thirty. It means *about* six-thirty—it means twenty minutes before seven, even fifteen minutes before— The lights at the corner changed, and two cabs came through. John would be in one of them. She knew John would be in one of them. She opened the door and stepped out, ready to run down the steps to John. Neither cab stopped.

It was six-forty-five. She went back into the house, and sat at the telephone table, and took a long, slow breath. She dialed a number. She heard the repeated signal of a ringing telephone. After a long time she replaced the receiver.

Something has happened to John, her mind said, the words formed carefully, distinctly in her mind. *Something has happened to John.* Something has happened—

172

She got up from the chair and went to the door and opened it and went down the steps outside, and went carefully because her whole body seemed to have grown numb. She stopped an empty cab and got into it and gave an address in a voice which was not her voice.

XIII

MILLER WOULD LISTEN; he did listen. He listened with patience, and let the patience show. But before Shapiro had finished, before he had nearly finished, Miller was shaking his head. He said, "The trouble with you, Nate, is you've got a tender heart. You're a good cop, but you've got a tender heart."

"The book—" Shapiro said, and Miller shook his head more firmly. He said Shapiro had told him about the book.

"What's got you, Nate," Miller said, "is this girl. All right, she's a nice girl. She's in love with him. They're a nice young couple, like people say. It goes right to that tender heart of yours. Like strawberries go to my stomach. And you break out with a rash, same as I do. Hayward killed the Titus girl. He killed the old woman. The D. A.'s satisfied, now we know who the girl was. And you come in and talk about a book, that maybe somebody's stolen from the public library. And you haven't any idea what's in the book, except it's about this Titus family."

"Only," Shapiro said, "maybe we'd get a lead on who gets the money." But he spoke sadly. "O.K.," he said. "The other way it's open and shut. Only—the old lady had a lot of money."

"I tell you," Miller said, "whyn't you leave that to his lawyer? Just work your own side of the street? You're off duty now. You go home to Rosie and tell Rosie about it. She's got a tender heart, same as you have. You play it that way, Nate."

"There's a hole in it," Shapiro said, his voice even sadder, more tired, than it had been. "And—somebody'll maybe try to patch the hole."

"Somebody," Miller said. "Always this somebody. This frame-up artist. Look, Nate. I like you. We all like you. You've got a tender heart. Whyn't you just look at what we've got?

175

Like I do. Like Martinelli does. Martinelli says it's all right, and he's got to take it to the jury. So, maybe there'll be somebody on the jury with a tender heart like yours."

Shapiro shrugged. The shrug gave it up.

"Now," Miller said. "Listen. He meets this Titus girl. Very pretty girl. He rents an apartment for her. Maybe he says he's going to marry her. But then this other girl comes along, and she's a pretty girl too. *And* a girl with a lot of money. *And* the boss's daughter."

"Hayward's got plenty of money," Shapiro said. "He made twenty thousand bail like snapping his fingers."

"All right," Miller said. "Let's keep it simple. Maybe what you and I'd call plenty of money, he wouldn't. But, keep it simple. He falls in love with Miss Phillips. But he's shacked up with the other girl. He says to the other girl, 'Honey, looks like it's all a mistake. I've found a girl I like better. Nice knowing you and here's a check. So you run back to auntie.'"

"Mrs. Piermont wasn't her aunt," Shapiro said, sadly. He was told he brought up the damnedest points. So, Mrs. Piermont wasn't auntie. What did that have to do with it?

"Nothing," Shapiro said. "So—the Titus girl gets sore. Says, wait until she tells this new girl of his a thing or two, and see how the new girl likes it."

"Sure you get it," Miller said. "That's what she says. He says, 'Now, honey, wait a minute. You wouldn't do a thing like that.' And she says—"

"All right," Shapiro said. "So he kills her so she can't spill her story."

"All worked up," Miller said. "Doesn't know what he's doing, hardly. Maybe doesn't really mean to kill her. Just scare her."

"The old lady?" Shapiro said. "Just because she came down when he was looking for the picture?"

"No," Miller said. "She could identify him. Seen him with the girl. Knew more about what was going on than she told him. Maybe she was waiting until she'd actually identified the Titus girl. Maybe—how the hell'd I know what a woman that old thinks? Anyway, he kills her." He paused. He was very patient. "What the hell do you want, Nate?" he said. "I've seen you ready to go with half as much."

Shapiro shrugged again. He said that Miller was the boss—Miller and the D. A. He said he just worked there. He said O.K., he'd go home to Rosie. Only, he said, it would be interesting to have them go over the slips and find out who last was interested in the Tituses of Rockland County, New York. Miller sighed deeply.

"Sure," he said. "Sure we will, Nate. Did I ever say we wouldn't?"

"You're bringing him in now?" Shapiro said.

"In the morning," Miller told him. "He won't try to run away, Nate. And, if he does, that'll be swell, won't it? That would toughen you up, wouldn't it?"

"It'd help," Shapiro said, and went out of Miller's office, and through the squadroom and out into the spring-bright street. He walked toward the subway which would take him home to Brooklyn, and to Rosie, who had a tender heart like his own. He would go home and walk the dog, and have a glass of wine with Rosie and after dinner they might go to a movie and— He even went halfway down the stairs to the subway platform.

And then, his face long with misery, he went back up the stairs and walked a block to a diner, and had a cup of coffee and a hamburger. He called Rosie up and said he would be a little late.

"Like always," Rose Shapiro said. "I should marry a policeman."

* * *

A sign in front of her said, "Sit back and relax." Barbara Phillips sat tightly erect; leaned forward a little. Her hands were clenched into fists, and one rested on either slender thigh. She seemed strained for sudden movement; her mouth was set so that generous lips were pressed hard together, narrowed by pressure. She willed the cab to speed greater than the cluttered street allowed; when the cab stopped, behind several other cars, for a distant red light, she tightened her lips further, so as not to scream—to scream, "Go on! Go *on!*"

But behind the desperate urgency in her mind, there was the deep darkness of hopelessness. It would be no good. It couldn't be any good. The telephone had rung and rung—it had shrilled its call in emptiness.

I'm not like this, Barbara thought. I've never been like this. I'm not this kind of fool—this kind of hysterical fool. Now, she thought, right now, he is going up our steps, ringing the doorbell. There was some little thing—some meaningless little thing. It was only that. He had trouble getting a cab. Or he got a cab and something happened to it—a tire. The motor stalled. Some of the cabs are old. Or—or something came up and he didn't have a chance to telephone. Or—something's happened to his telephone. Or—

I should go back, she thought. I should go back and sit very quietly and wait for him to come. And if he doesn't come, it means—it means he's been arrested. He said that—that he'd be there unless they decided to arrest him. We thought of that. There's an answer to that.

But the answer was not the one she had made—was making. It was not to go numbly into a cab and give the address of an apartment in which he could not be, and to sit thus, frantic with fear—driven by urgency without meaning.

"Take it easy, lady," the driver said. "Get there as fast as we can. Traffic's bad, lady."

But she had not spoken. Surely she had not spoken—had not cried out, "Go faster. *Faster!*" It must be, she thought, that I am screaming so loudly, in silence, that he can feel me screaming.

"I know," she said. "I realize that, driver."

"Just take it easy," the driver said again, and she realized he had been watching her in the mirror. She forced herself to lean back in the seat. But in a second she was sitting as before. The cab was moving again—moving slowly, creeping. It moved to the center of the street and stopped for a left turn. There was no end to the traffic which opposed them, through which he could not turn. There would never—

There was a gap. The driver went through it. In mid-block, he pulled to the curb. He said, "See? Didn't take so long, after all."

There was no measure of the time it had taken. She gave him a bill without looking at it, and shook her head—shook it with a kind of violence—when he reached into his pocket for change. She was out of the cab and into the building, and the driver sat and looked at her, and still held the bill in his hand.

The elevator was not at the lobby floor; the elevator was closed blankly against her. She put her finger hard on the signal button, and pressed hard, and held her finger there, pressing. After what seemed a long time—but still there was no measure of time—she heard the elevator moving in the shaft. It moved with lumbering slowness. Finally, she heard it stop behind the gate, and then the gate opened. A man in a uniform coat looked out at her, reproachfully. He said, "All right all right. Must be in an awful hurry."

"I'm sorry," she said. "It's—Mr. Hayward. He's on the fifth floor." She went into the elevator.

"Hayward?" he said, and looked at her curiously. "You said Mr. Hayward?"

"Yes," she said. "Yes—please."

"Fifth floor," he said, and closed the elevator door, and the car went up. It went slowly, lumberingly. The man kept his hand on the controls, but turned and looked at her. He did not say anything more, but he looked at her with unhidden curiosity. She was only half conscious of this, and urged the car upward. It was as if she were lifting the car.

The car stopped and the door opened.

"Second door, that way," the man said, gesturing, and after she had left the elevator, walked the way he had indicated, stopped at the second door, he stood just outside the elevator car and watched her. But then, as she began to press on the

179

doorbell button, he went back into the car and, dimly, she heard the door clang shut.

She heard the bell ringing inside the apartment, and took her finger from the button, and for a second waited. But then she pressed hard, again, on the button, and heard the bell— but really it was a buzzer—answer from inside. It seemed to answer angrily. She took her finger from the button and listened, and felt coldness creeping over her; felt defeat cry in her throat. Once more, but dully now, without anticipation, she lifted her hand so that her finger was on the button of the buzzer.

But then, before she could press the button, she heard movement on the other side of the door. The movement became the sound of someone walking, slowly, toward the door. Then the door opened.

"John!" she said. "Why—*John!*"

She looked up at him, and her face was bright; a kind of brightness flooded through her.

And there was nothing in his eyes.

He said, "Hello," as if the word meant nothing. She felt the word, strangely, as she would have felt a blow. The brightness went out of her face, and out of her mind.

"John?" she said. "I—I waited. I—"

"I'm sorry," he said, in the same expressionless voice. "I— something came up, Barbara."

He seemed now to speak very slowly, using each simple word carefully, as if he were not quite sure of it. And he did not step aside to let her into the apartment.

"Don't you—?" she began, and stopped and began again. "Father told me something," she said. "Something—important. Are you—did you want me to—just wait?" She looked at him again, and now his eyes were not so blank. There was something hidden in his eyes. "Has something happened?" she said.

"Happened?" he said. "No, nothing's happened. I—" He stopped, and she saw—thought she saw—the faintest negative motion of his head. But then she saw a curious rigidity in his whole body, in the way he stood. "I got held up," he said. "I was just leaving. Why don't you—" But he did not finish. "Fact is," he said, "I—had a drink or two. Didn't realize it was so—"

He still spoke slowly, with exaggerated care, as if the words he used were elusive, alien. And there was still something hidden in his eyes. It was as if John Hayward—the reality of John Hayward—were hidden in his eyes.

"I—" she said. "Of course, John."

She spoke dully, and continued to look at him—continued to try to find him in his eyes, in his face. This can't be happening, she thought. *Can't* be happening. Can't—

She felt herself, her whole body, moving—swaying—from side to side. She felt that she had been struck, and that the blow had left a kind of numbness—almost a kind of dizziness.

"It's all right," she heard him say, as if from a long way off. But then she felt his hand on her arm, steadying her. And then he stepped back from the door, opening it further as he did so, and the hand on her arm pressed, just perceptibly, moving her toward the open door. She went with him into the apartment.

Sunlight came through windows at the end of the living room, and was hard, rectangular, on the floor. The sunlight seemed to leave the rest of the room dim. It was a long room, not wide. There were two doors in the right wall of the living room.

I was never here before, she thought, and realized that she had spoken, aloud, the meaningless words, only when he said, "No. You never were." And then he said, still speaking in the same meaningless fashion, "I'm sorry, Barbara. Sorry about— all of it. I guess you made a mistake."

"A mistake?" she said. "What do you mean? John—*what's happened to you, John?*"

"Just—run down," he said. "Things piled up and—well, I had a drink. Then I had another drink. I guess—"

"I tried the telephone," she said. "It rang—and rang. You didn't answer it? Heard it and—didn't answer it?"

"Yes," he said. "I guess that's it."

She put her hands over her face; pressed the tips of her fingers hard against her forehead. Her voice was muffled by her hands.

"You knew I was waiting," she said. "Instead of coming to me, you had a drink? And when the telephone rang you didn't answer it? Although you must have known I'd—"

"That's the way it was," he said. "I—I guess you were wrong about me. You'd better—maybe you'd better go along home. Figure the whole thing was—"

She had taken her hands down from her face. She looked up at him.

"That's the way it is," he said. His voice was suddenly strained, harsh. "You'd better go along home."

***

In the first place, Shapiro thought, Miller was probably right. There isn't anybody else in it—no "frame-up artist." The chances are a hundred to one there isn't anybody else. Killings are simple things; simpler than anything else. If you want to run a swindle, you plan it all out, and take your time to get things right. If you want to rob a bank, you case the bank, and you don't hurry, even if it takes you weeks. You get it all right first, so there won't be a slip-up. But if you're going to kill somebody, you just go out and kill him. There isn't a lot of rigmarole. Killing is a simple thing. So, there isn't anybody else. Hayward killed them both. Why don't I go home and walk the dog?

In the second place, even suppose there is somebody, why would he do anything else? He's done all he needs to do. Tomorrow we take Hayward in, and in a few weeks—or maybe a few months—we try him. Martinelli handles it, and Martinelli's good. They bring up all this about somebody impersonating Hayward and the jury says, "Ho-hum," and doesn't recommend mercy, because it was a girl he killed—a girl maybe in love with him—and an old lady. What would this

182

other guy need to do now? He's done plenty. (Walk the dog and have a glass of wine and something fit to eat.)

Shapiro waited for a bus, his face a drooping pattern of discouragement. The bus came. He got on the bus, which took him in a direction opposite to the direction of Brooklyn. (Rosie would say, "You're tired, Nate. Everything they put on you, Nate.")

In the third place—in the third place, maybe this man—the man who had stolen the book from the library because, if you looked carefully, you'd find his name in it—was one of those who didn't know enough to stop. He hadn't heard Miller. He didn't know Martinelli figured the D. A.'s office had all it needed. And—perhaps he did know that, up in Hawthorne, they hadn't held Hayward. Perhaps he'd called up and said he was a lawyer named Still and found out that, after all the trouble he'd gone to, Hayward was on the loose again. And—perhaps he was a lawyer named Still. For a man's lawyer to call up was legitimate, whatever he really called about.

The bus stopped at Thirty-sixth and Fifth and Shapiro got off. He moved, dispiritedly, eastward. He'd just have a look around, and there wouldn't be anything to find, and he'd go home. (Only, by now, Rosie would have walked the dog.)

He went into the apartment house. The elevator was at the lobby floor. The operator said, "Oh, it's you again," and Shapiro said, "That's right." Then he said, "Mr. Hayward got company?"

"Girl went up. You want to go up?"

For answer, Shapiro got into the elevator. The operator closed the door with a bang.

"Just now?" Shapiro said.

"Quite a while ago," the man said, which left Nathan Shapiro uncertain whether "quite a while" meant hours or minutes. It probably didn't matter. He wasn't going to get anywhere.

"Suppose," Shapiro said, "you let me off at the fourth. I'll walk the rest."

XIV

SHE CONTINUED to look at him, to look into his strange, blank eyes. He repeated it, in the same harsh voice: "You'd better go home." He said, "There's nothing you can do."

For seconds, she merely looked at him; looked at him, and tried to find him.

"No," she said then. "Not until you tell me what's happened. What it's all about."

Her voice was quite clear, now, and quite steady. Her body was no longer trembling.

"You want it spelled out," he said. "That's what you want?"

"Yes," she said. "That's what I want, John."

He shook his head, just perceptibly. For an instant, his eyes were no longer blank; for that instant it seemed as if blankness he was desperately maintaining in his eyes had parted, as curtains might part although they were drawn tight against stirring air. But the blankness returned so quickly that she could not be sure it had ever broken.

"It ought to be obvious," he said. "There's nothing you can do. You made a mistake." He paused. "What it comes to," he said, "you backed the wrong horse."

"No," she said. "I don't believe that. That doesn't spell it out."

"Oh," he said, "I appreciate it. Everything you tried. You're a nice girl. Go home. You're better off at home." He paused again. She looked at his hands, and saw them clenched. "Safer," he said.

"You appreciate it," she said. "Did you really say that? To me? You *appreciate* what I've done?" He nodded. "What's the matter with you?" she said. "*What's the matter with you?*"

He moved. He had been standing with his back to the windows. He turned a little, and now she could, as he stood in profile toward the windows, see more clearly the fixed blankness in his face.

"All right," he said. "They're too many for me. There are too many of them and they're too good." He spoke, now, more loudly than he had spoken before. "Do you hear me?" he said, in the loud, harsh voice. "I can't get away with it."

"Get away with it?" she said. She looked up into his blank eyes, and again thought the blankness wavered for an instant.

"I needed a drink," he said, still loudly. "You know how it is, sometimes, when you have a drink? The fuzz rubs off. Everything gets all clear. You can't fool yourself any more. I had a couple of drinks—maybe I had three or four drinks. I said, 'It's no good. They've got you.' So—"

"You're sick," she said. "That's what's the matter."

"No," he said. "Maybe a little drunk. Drunk enough to get things clear. It's no good. Why don't you get out of here? Go off and—get over it. Because—"

"No," she said. "You'll have to say it."

"That I did what they say? All right. I'll—"

But he broke off. He turned quickly and crossed the narrow room to a desk against the wall, between the doors. He sat at the desk and wrote, rapidly, with a fountain pen on a sheet of paper. She watched his back, could see his moving hand. He wrote very briefly. He came back and stood by her, and had moved violently.

"Spell it out," he said. "You wanted it spelled out, didn't you? Spell it out and sign it. Better than just telling you. Write it down and sign it."

She waited. And now, again, her body trembled.

"Listen," John Hayward said. "Read it to you." He was almost shouting in the harsh voice. "Reads this way: 'I killed Julie Titus because she tried to shake me down. I killed the old lady—'"

He stopped suddenly. He held the paper out to her.

"See?" he said. "All signed. Read it. Barbara—*read it!*"

Her hands were numb; her body was numb. She held out a numb hand and took the paper.

186

What he had read was not written on the paper. There were four words on the paper. They wavered on the paper. They came clear on the paper.

"For God's sake go."

"All right," he said, quickly and loudly. "That's the way it is. That's what I am. Get out before something else—"

His eyes were alive, now. They leapt with life. She looked up from the words on the sheet of paper, and his eyes seemed frighteningly alive—and demanding.

She made her face quiet, tightened her trembling lips against an answer.

"All right," she said, and made her voice expressionless. "I'll go, John. I'll—" She turned away. Her mind swirled. She took a few steps, moving through danger vibrating in the air, but yet not to be understood. She started to put the paper on a table near the center of the living room.

There were drinking glasses on the table. There were *two* glasses on the table.

For an instant her whole body seemed to freeze. She could not complete even the simple action of putting the paper down on the table. She stood staring at the glasses—stood too long, and knew she stood too long, and could not, for seconds, force herself to put the paper on the table. Then she put it there, and there was a sound and she turned, her back to the table, her numb hands on it.

John had moved near her, although she had not heard him. And one of the doors she faced was open. A man stood there, with the light behind him, so that his face was shadowed. Standing so, he might have been John Hayward—or any other quite ordinary-looking man. But he had a revolver in his right hand.

"Silly thing to forget, Johnny," the man—a man she had never seen before, but had seen everywhere—said in a light, rather pleasant voice. "Tough on the young lady the finesse didn't work. But that's the way—"

He raised the revolver. In that same instant, John leaped, not toward the man in the doorway across the room, but toward Barbara Phillips. He was between her and the man in the door. His body jarred hard against hers, and his arms came around her as he made himself a wall between her and the slowly pointing revolver in the man's hand.

In that instant, she did not breathe, and then there was a violent noise in the room and she felt John's body leap convulsively against her, and then whirl away. She could, then, see the man in the doorway. He was looking at his empty hand. Ridiculously, as if he had bruised a finger, he shook a shattered hand, and blood splattered from it to the carpet.

"All right, mister," a weary, a sad, voice said from the end of the living room—from the door between the living room and the outside corridor. "If you hold it up, it won't bleed so much."

A tall man came sadly into the room. He shook his head.

"Not the shot I used to be," he said. "Should just have hit the gun."

She was shaking. She was swallowing, convulsively, against something rising in her throat. She looked at John.

"That's right," John said. "You never met Mr. Woodson, did you, Barbara? Mr. Pit Woodson? Mr. P. I. T., for Peter Irving Titus, Woodson?" He looked at Woodson. "I'm afraid," John said, slowly, "that Mr. Woodson can't offer to shake hands." He turned to Shapiro, then.

"And where the hell," John said in a strange voice, "did you come from, Mr. Shapiro?"

***

Pit Woodson had been waiting in the apartment when, at about five-thirty, after garaging the car, John had let himself into it. Woodson had already made himself a drink, and in all respects comfortable. He had come to persuade John to write a "nice little confession."

"With this, Johnny," Woodson had said, and waggled the revolver. "Make yourself a drink, Johnny. Good, stiff drink." He had waggled the revolver again, and John had made himself a drink. "Sit down, Johnny," Woodson had said, and once more waggled the revolver, and John had sat down. Like the rest of it, the last had had a certain dream-like quality.

"So the 'T' stands for Titus," John had said, and took a swallow of his drink and Pit had said, "That's smart of you, Johnny," and drank from his own glass.

"I told him," John said to Barbara, "that he had gone a long way around and—believe it or not—he went into a little discussion of how you had to plan your whole strategy from the first card you played. Told me that that was what had been wrong with my bridge. Speaking of me in the past tense."

"Past perfect," Barbara said.

They were back at Monet's, side by side on a banquette in a corner. They were not particularly hungry and John, certainly, was not thirsty—he had actually had three stiff drinks while waiting for Pit Woodson to get around to killing him— but Monet's, particularly in the evening, was a quiet place. They needed a quiet place.

"The plan was what we thought," John said. "He let me go over it, and agreed to all of it. He had chosen me because— well, he said, 'You fitted the bill, Johnny.' He made something of a point of having nothing against me personally. I went into a lot of detail—to postpone being killed—and he let me talk and kept saying, 'Smart of you, Johnny.' "

John paused. He looked at the drink he had hardly tasted, and shook his head at it.

"I'm afraid," he said, "I didn't give you any credit, Barbara. I didn't think credit would—do you any good. Under the circumstances."

"You were to write the confession and then—then kill yourself? I mean, seem to have killed yourself?"

That had been the plan. Woodson had been almost apologetic about it. He had, however, been quite reasonable. Johnny—the implication of "good old Johnny" was in the tone —would see how it was. The police wouldn't see the obvious, and act on it. He couldn't himself, see what they had been waiting for. Or, specifically, why they had turned John loose at Hawthorne. He had, frankly, considered this damn' inefficient of the police.

"My God, Johnny," Pit Woodson said, "I gave them enough. Wouldn't you say I'd given them enough?"

He had seemed, John said, to seek sympathy for the trouble he'd gone to, and the lack of appreciation the police had shown. "Actually," John said. "That's the way he sounded."

But Woodson had kept the revolver very ready. When the telephone had rung, he had shaken his head and moved the gun from side to side. And time had begun to run out. Finally, Woodson had said that this was all very well, but they'd better get on with it.

"Just write it that you killed them," Woodson said. "Just do that, Johnny."

"I asked him why I should," John said. "Since, to make the confession any good, he would have to kill me anyway. He was good enough to say I had a point there."

"He's—unbelievable," Barbara said. At that, John shook his head. He said he had, in the last few days, learned to believe the unbelievable without half trying.

"You know," he said, "I still feel that I've been turned upside down. Things aren't—I'm not sure of the order of things, any more."

"You thought the world was domesticated," she said. "At bottom. Oh—that there was anger and violence, and terrible great quarrels, but that things are predictable. Most men do. Why would you sign a confession, if he was going to kill you anyway? Would you have?"

John didn't know. On the whole, he thought he might have. You played for time—for minutes, down to seconds. Something might happen—while you stayed alive. Of course, something had.

"You rang the doorbell," John told her. "That was what happened."

John had been told to get rid of whoever it was. He had tried. Woodson had moved to the door of the bedroom, and stood there with the revolver on John. "And," John said, "on you. As you came in, he closed the door—almost closed it. What I tried—well, it's pretty obvious what I tried."

"Because," she said, "he'd have had to kill me, too. Make it appear—oh, that I'd found out, that you'd killed me, and then confessed and killed yourself?"

John didn't see what else Woodson could have done, being Woodson. He would have had to try—well, to drop the outstanding trumps. John had managed, letting Barbara in, to leave the apartment door on latch, just on the chance. The chance had been—

"Look," Barbara said, and indicated with her head. She indicated a tall man, who seemed to droop, who was standing near the door and looked around the dimly lit room. He saw what he was looking for, and came toward them.

"Evening, Miss Phillips," Shapiro said, unhappily. "Mr. Hayward. Miller'd like to see you, Mr. Hayward."

They looked at him. John half rose.

"Oh," Shapiro said. "No hurry about it. Just like to fill in a few things. About what Mr. Woodson told you—things like that. Any time tomorrow that's convenient."

For a moment, John remained, as if frozen, half standing, half not.

"It will have to be in the morning," Barbara Phillips said. "Because tomorrow afternoon we have to go to the Municipal Building." John, still in his odd crouch, looked at her. "To get the license," Barbara said.

John looked at her. He looked at Nathan Shapiro.

"Mr. Shapiro," John Hayward said, "can I please buy you a drink?"

Shapiro thought he might, so long as he made it wine.

"Anything stronger," Shapiro said, "upsets my stomach."